SHE LOOKED TRULY SHOCKED AS SHE NODDED HER HEAD IN AGREEMENT.

"LATINA, 'ME, TOGETHER, YOU, GO?'"

CHARACTERS

RUDOLF SCHMIDT
FRIEND NUMBER 2. COULD THIS TALL BOY BE FOND OF LATINA?

CHLOE SCHNEIDER
LATINA'S NUMBER-ONE FRIEND. A GALLANT YOUNG GIRL WHO ACTS AS THE LEADER OF THE GROUP OF CHILDREN.

LATINA
A YOUNG DEVIL GIRL ADOPTED BY DALE. SHE'S EARNEST, KIND, AND CLEVER, BUT ALSO SURPRISINGLY STUBBORN.

ANTHONY HOFFMANN
FRIEND NUMBER 4. A SLIM, SMART YOUNG BOY.

MARCEL BAKER
FRIEND NUMBER 3. A BAKER'S SON. SLIGHTLY PLUMP.

If It's For My Daughter, I'd Even Defeat a Demon Lord

Volume 1

CHIROLU

Illustrator: Truffle

IF IT'S FOR MY DAUGHTER, I'D EVEN DEFEAT A DEMON LORD: VOLUME 1
by CHIROLU

Translated by Matthew Warner
Edited by Sasha McGlynn

Copyright © 2015 CHIROLU
Illustrations by Truffle

First published in Japan in 2015 by Hobby Japan, Tokyo.
Publication rights for this English edition arranged through Hobby Japan, Tokyo.

Find more books like this one at www.j-novel.club!

President and Publisher: Samuel Pinansky
Managing Editor: Aimee Zink

ISBN: 978-1-7183-5300-8
Printed in Korea
First Printing: April 2019
10 9 8 7 6 5 4 3 2 1

Contents

When you were born, there was a large rainbow spread across the sky.

That's right. Regardless of how their language and culture may differ, all "people" say that a rainbow is made of seven colors. That's because the rainbow is a fragment of those great beings that control the will of the world, the gods. They exist as seven beings, which is why they're called the "Gods of the Seven Colors."

The Red God, Ahmar, is the god of war. He's also the god of arbitration and judgment. If you're ever in trouble, then you should visit his temple.

The Orange God, Quirmizi, is the god of the harvest. Right, we went to a festival together, didn't we? One held in the hopes that many crops would grow.

The Yellow God, Asfar, is the god of education and leaders. Many people gather at his temple in order to learn. You're a smart one, so it might be good for you to study there, as well.

Travelers gather under the Green God, Akhdar. That's right. The world is incredibly vast. It's absolutely brimming with things that you've never seen before.

The Blue God, Azraq, is the god of business. When you become an adult, I wonder what sort of job you'll have.

The Indigo God, Niili, rules over life and death, as well as the study of diseases and medicine. Magic doesn't work on illnesses, so be sure to take care.

As the leader of the gods, the Violet God, Banafsaj, rules over creation and destruction, as well as reincarnation.

Rainbows appear in the sky when the gods are looking down over the land.

You were born with the gods watching over you, so you'll be fine.

You'll definitely be happy. That's all that I want.

It's alright.

See, there's a rainbow. You're protected by fate.

Please, please be happy.

From now on, I'll be watching over you from the other side of the rainbow, as well.

1: The Young Man and the Little Girl Meet

There was a young man walking through the depths of the forest. Even though the sun was still out, this forest, untouched by humans, remained dim and gloomy. Aside from the occasional chirping of birds, there were no sounds to be heard. The place definitely had an oppressive atmosphere to it.

With a look of great displeasure on his face, the man glanced down at the sword in his hand.

"Ugh, damn it…" he spat, wiping his blade off on some nearby grass. The sword was absolutely coated with a foul-smelling mucus. "*This* is why nobody wanted to take this job… Man, I'm gonna need to wash myself off or something before heading back." When he saw the mucus was stuck to his leather coat as well, the look on his face grew even more pained.

It hadn't been long since he'd gotten to the forest, having taken on a request to cull the frog-like magical beasts that had overpopulated it. While the task itself wasn't much trouble, as he had confidence in handling both his weapon and magic, the trip here and back was time-consuming.

"I took it on since I had time until my next job, but… I guess this was a mistake, huh?" Hearing the *splish, splash* of his own sticky footsteps on the grass, he let out a sigh and drooped his shoulders.

The main reason he'd taken on this job was because he could make the round trip from and back to the town he was currently based out of within the course of a day. He cursed himself for having made the decision so lightly.

The work itself hadn't really been anything of note. It had been easy for him to find the colony the magical beasts had made in the depths of the forest, and wiping them out had been simple as well. If only he hadn't gotten coated in their bodily fluids and the mucus they spat up. The only saving grace was that the horrible stench had quickly numbed his sense of smell. But if he returned to town like this, even the gatekeepers he was friends with would be taken aback.

In the town he was currently based out of, he was making something of a name for himself as an adventurer. He had just turned 18, the age at which one was considered an adult in this country, but back in his home town, he had been treated as though he'd come of age ever since he turned 15. Because he'd decided on this occupation back then, he'd been able to build up a few years' worth of achievements and earn a reputation beyond what his youth would imply.

His hair was black with a bit of light brown mixed in, and he wore a long coat made of magical beast leather. On his left arm was a magical device gauntlet. Those were the outward traits that people would use to describe the man named Dale Reki.

"Oh water, by my name, I order you to heed my call. 《Search: Water》" He recited this spell, and his magic activated. Sensing the strong presence of water, Dale changed his route and pushed his way through an animal trail.

As his field of vision cleared, he saw a small river running before him. Having found what he was seeking, Dale breathed a sigh of relief.

He took off his coat and plunged it into the gushing water. This one good coat of his was endowed with magic, so the mass of mucus

11

washed away. Because it repelled water, it would soon be dry, so Dale hung it on a nearby branch to air out.

He stopped and thought for a moment. Dale looked over his body again and remembered the unpleasant smell and mucus. Thinking that he should wash himself thoroughly, he took off his stab-resistant tunic. He could afford to act so confidently because he knew the magical beasts and other animals in the forest proved no threat to him.

His coat dried quickly enough, but his tunic and pants were still dripping wet. And so, Dale started a campfire, sat down on his spread-out coat in just his underwear, and began cooking the fish he'd caught while he'd bathed in the river.

By the time the savory smell wafted through the air around him, his clothes had mostly dried. Keeping his eyes on the fish, Dale quickly slipped on his clothes. After all, he wasn't quite bold enough to enjoy a meal in his underwear in a place like this.

That was when he heard a rustling sound.

He figured it was a small animal drawn by the smell of his meal, but when he looked, he was shocked.

A small child was staring at him from the other side of the thicket, with their tiny head just barely peeking out from a bush.

At first, Dale was surprised that he'd misread the presence he'd felt. Then, he was bewildered that he'd found a child aimlessly wandering around a forest filled with magical beasts. It was when he was thinking that there shouldn't be any villages around here that he realized something: there were curved, black horns on top of the child's head.

A devil, huh…? What a pain… He mentally clicked his tongue.

Devils were an insular group, and they possessed the greatest abilities out of the seven races. As for distinguishing physical traits, devils had horns on the top of their heads.

Should I kill her...? He figured that would be the quickest way to deal with this. Devils were nothing but trouble, after all.

Dale grasped the handle of his sword tight... and then let go. He'd just finished washing himself off, and he didn't want blood splattering all over him. It was only a quick thought, but that was his reasoning.

Looking like she was about to break out in tears, the girl kept her big grey eyes fixed right on him.

Having let go of his sword, Dale calmed himself down enough to observe the child, and that was when he finally realized why he felt so uneasy when he first saw her: one of the devil girl's horns was broken off at the base.

Seriously? A kid like this is a criminal...?

Taken aback by this realization, Dale cringed at how ridiculous that would be. In the past, a fellow adventurer had told him one of the devils' customs:

Devils considered their horns sacred, as they were symbols of their race. So when a devil committed a crime, one of their horns was broken off, and the criminal was exiled.

Even knowing that, Dale couldn't help but have questions. After all, the child before him was far too young to be capable of a crime. Devils had lifespans far longer than humans like Dale, and while he didn't know if human ages were equal to theirs, the height of the girl staring at him from within the bushes made Dale guess that she was about five or six. She most certainly didn't look old enough to be capable of making her own judgments.

Dale suddenly remembered the fish in his campfire when he realized that the devil child was glancing at it, and he hurriedly pulled out the skewer. It had gotten a little burnt.

"Hmm…"

As he moved the skewer left and right, the child's gaze followed. It seemed he hadn't imagined it; she appeared to be quite interested in the fish as well.

"…Do you want some?"

He'd feel bad about eating in front of her, like he was flaunting his meal. And because of that thought, he called out to the girl almost without thinking. At the same time, he dumbfoundedly wondered what he was saying.

When she heard Dale speak, the child's gaze moved from the fish back to his face, and she tilted her head slightly.

"***? ***, ****?"

"Huh? Um…?" Now it was Dale's turn to tilt his head. It was too quick for him to follow along, but he felt like he had heard that language somewhere before. "Hmm, if I remember right…" He dragged out the words of the fellow adventurer who had taught him about devils from the depths of his memory. "He said that the language of the devils was the same as the one used in spells, right…?"

He decided that was it.

Spells were words used to utilize the power of the phenomenon known as magic. The number of people who could employ spells was limited; it wasn't like everyone could use such words. But devils were apt at speaking them, and thus able to use them as their mother tongue. That was precisely why it was said that devils were all "natural-born magic users."

"Hmm, then… 'Come, beside, need, this?'"

From the language used in spells, Dale picked out vocabulary that seemed like it would convey the meaning he wanted. He'd never intended to use the words to hold a conversation, so he hadn't the slightest idea how to do so correctly.

When she heard his words, a clear look of relief appeared on the girl's face. With a rustling sound, she moved through the thicket and drew closer.

Even though he had been the one who had called out, Dale was once more left speechless.

It wasn't just because the child had approached a complete stranger without a hint of caution.

It was also because she was so terribly thin.

What he could see of her limbs peeking out from under the old rag that must have once been a one-piece dress was nothing but skin and bones. He could tell at a glance that she was suffering from malnutrition. It wouldn't even take a sword to end her life—if he wrapped his hands around her too-thin neck, it would be easy to snap it before she could even try to resist.

While devils kept away from outsiders, they were also a race known to have strong bonds amongst themselves. That was precisely why they regarded exile as such a harsh punishment. Furthermore, while long-lived, devils had a very low birth rate; they were said to cherish children like treasure.

Dale hadn't even considered the possibility that such a young child would be forced to face such harsh exile, even if they actually *were* being treated as a criminal.

"Come on, eat. Ah, no matter what I say, you won't understand…"

Dale grinned wide and thrust the skewer towards her. Magic spells didn't use words like "eat up." But even though Dale had handed the girl the skewer, she simply looked down at it, then back at him.

"******?"

"It's fine, so just eat."

The girl looked at Dale, as if trying to size him up. For the time being, he responded with a nod, and she slowly brought the fish to her mouth.

Bit by bit, she nibbled away at it with small bites. As he had nothing else to do, Dale simply sat there and watched, and all the while, he thought about how she looked just like a small animal.

While he waited for her to finish eating the fish, Dale once more searched for words to use.

"Ah… 'Person, protect, you, exist?'"

It's not like it was certain just yet that the child didn't have a guardian. Carefully watching Dale and listening to his awkward wording, she replied even more slowly than she had before.

"***, ************, ****. *** *********, ********"

"Hmm… Together, not, here? …Beasts, reject…?"

Dale was only able to pick up broken fragments of meaning, but the expression on the girl's face was decidedly grim. After thinking a bit, she grabbed Dale's hand in her tiny grasp and pulled him along.

Following as the girl continued through the forest step by tiny step, Dale continued to ponder the matter.

Now that I think about it, it was just a sudden impulse that made me call out to her and give her the fish. What exactly do I intend to do next?

Suddenly, the child stopped. Looking doubtful, she looked up at Dale.

"What? Up ahead?"

She pointed forward and shook her head.

"************"

"'Beasts,' again? …And 'not,' is it?"

While thinking about what that meant, Dale stepped in the direction the child was pointing.

"…!" And then, he stopped dead in his tracks.

Even someone like Dale, who made his living by the sword, couldn't keep looking at the thing that was once a person lying before him.

…This is a devil, right? From the shape of the horns, a… male?

It was impossible to tell when he had died, and the cause of death wasn't clear, either. The wounds were simply too severe. There were so many magical beasts and animals in this forest that it was too hard to even tell if he had been attacked or if his body was torn apart after he died.

Both of his horns… are still there… Is he the kid's father? It's not like you could just abandon your exiled child and leave them all alone, after all.

Was it alright to feel relieved about that? He thought back to the girl's words from earlier. Connecting them together, it was most likely her father's final order.

"You mustn't stay by my body. Before long, beasts will gather here. And a small child alone could not defend themselves against something like that."

"Ah, damn it. Now that I've seen this, I can't just leave her alone…" Dale vigorously scratched his head with both hands.

He'd pieced together the father's dying wishes.

Even if the devil girl had indeed followed her father's orders and not stayed by his side, she had still managed to survive in that very forest until Dale found her.

"Oh you who belong to the earth, by my name, I order you shift according to my wishes. 《Ground Transfiguration》" Dale recited as he touched his hand to the ground next to the body. The earth suddenly caved in, leaving behind a single hole.

Perhaps because she had heard his spell, the girl had drawn close to Dale's side and was looking at him timidly. Dale looked straight at her and spoke.

"Let's at least give him a burial. …Do you get it? Um… 'Inter, earth, death, person.'"

After reflecting on his words, the girl suddenly gave a single nod. Dale worried for a moment about whether or not it was alright to let a kid see a body in such a horrible state, but this one seemed to have long since accepted the reality of the situation. As if she was saying her final farewells, the child stared straight at her "father," not looking away for a second.

Perhaps she had come to check on him now and again.

The girl simply watched as Dale placed the body in the hole, then once more used magic to fill it.

"*****"

"You're saying thanks? Don't worry about it."

Dale once again cast his spell, this time above the grave that he had just finished creating. Summoned by his earth magic, a pure-white megalith appeared there. It was hastily made and he was unable to carve a name into it, but it was at least a proper grave now.

"Hmm… well, I guess this is fate, huh?"

Standing behind the girl, who was still staring intently at the grave, Dale let out a sigh.

19

"My name, 'Dale.' 'You, name?'"

She turned around with a somewhat surprised look on her face.

"Latina" was the single word of response that she gave.

"Latina, is it? Latina, 'Me, together, you, go?'"

She looked truly shocked as she nodded her head in agreement.

Looking once more at Latina, Dale saw she was only wearing clothes that looked like rags, broken-down shoes, and a silver bracelet, which looked to be made for an adult and was far too big for her. It really was impressive that the girl had been able to survive like this. She was definitely lucky that it happened to be such a mild season.

When he buried Latina's father, Dale had looked for anything that could have helped tell him about where they had come from, but he wasn't able to find anything of note. He thought that at the very least, he'd like to give this child some sort of memento of her real father.

"Hmm, if I let Latina walk, then the sun will end up setting…" Dale said to himself while looking down at her, realizing that her stride wasn't even equal to half of his own. And considering the state she was in, it was hard to imagine that the girl would have much strength left in her tiny body.

"Guess I have no choice…"

Dale reached down and scooped Latina up into his arms, shocking the devil child once more. Her eyes already looked big, but now they were even more pronounced.

Latina calmly settled into Dale's arms, not struggling at all.

"You're so light!" She was so thin and lightweight that Dale blurted that out without even thinking. "Are you really going to be okay…?" Despite the ugly thoughts he had when they first met, he was still able to voice such concern. Dale wasn't a "bad" person to begin with, and ever since he'd decided to take care of the girl, he had become mentally attached enough to worry about her.

"You don't even have any belongings. We should hurry on back…"

Dale hurriedly recited some earth magic to confirm which direction he was heading, then quickly rushed back towards town.

†

The town that Dale was currently based out of was called "Kreuz."

As the name implied, it was a town that formed a slightly misshapen cross, and it served as an important point for traffic heading from the port towards the capital. Furthermore, as it was near the habitats of many magical beasts, it was also a place where those known as adventurers, who survived by their skill alone, tended to gather. In terms of commerce, it was the second-greatest city in the country of Laband. That was the town of Kreuz.

Its hospitality towards travelers was also considered a highlight of the town; it was because Kreuz welcomed visiting merchants that it was able to grow. And by utilizing the money it earned from those travelers as rewards for adventurers, the town was able to defend against the threat of magical beasts.

Kreuz was truly a town for travelers.

The town was also surrounded by thick walls with gates that faced the four cardinal directions and gatekeepers stationed at each one. People were allowed to enter the town by paying a toll.

Dale had arrived at the south gate, which was the one he usually used. When the gatekeeper, whom he was acquainted with, saw him, he gave him a confused look.

"Here's my toll for two."

"Huh? What's with the kid? ...A devil?" the middle-aged gatekeeper asked while checking the coins he was handed, his gaze fixed on the young child in Dale's arms all the while.

"I found her in the forest. Seems her dad died. ...Is there some sort of issue with me taking care of her?"

"Well, if you're gonna be responsible for 'er, then that's fine. You're going to check in with the Dancing Ocelot, right?"

"Yeah."

"Then it's fine." After frankly stating that, the gatekeeper let Dale and Latina through, then turned to face the next passerby. His reaction was just what Dale had expected. He knew his own name held a certain amount of clout, after all.

He slipped through the gate into the southern section of town, which held the residential quarters and traveler-centric shops side by side. This was where Dale spent most of his time. He had no use for the elevated northern section and its nobles or the high-end residential area in the west. He did occasionally visit the eastern section, though, with its concentration of marketplaces and shops, as well as quarters for merchants.

Ahmar was the principal deity for the country of Laband, and as such, the color red was valued highly there. That was clear just by looking at the streets of Kreuz. For example, the walls of the rows of buildings were built out of gray stones that were then painted and plastered many different hues, but nearly all of the roofs were a vivid red. Not only was it a way of requesting that the buildings themselves be granted the gods' divine protection, it was also said to be a way of telling the gods high up in the heavens that that was where their humble servants were.

Though this may have been the rougher part of ʋ
still bustling with energy. It was around the time when the
setting, so there were people hurrying home, looking for loʋ
for the night, wanting to spend the day's earnings on food and boʋ
selling food to travelers… A great number of people of all sorts were
coming and going through the area.

In Dale's arms, Latina was unable to remain calm, and while
her eyes darted all over, there was no panic or fear on her face,
just pure curiosity. The child's cheeks were slightly flushed, and
occasionally her eyes opened wide enough that they were practically
circles. Latina seemed to be quite interested in the great number of
people she saw about the town.

"This is the street…" While it was meant for Latina, Dale knew
that the meaning wasn't getting across, so he said it to himself
instead.

"***? Dale."

"Man, it sure is inconvenient that we can't communicate…"

Dale kept on walking, thinking Latina would at least need to
learn the language of the western continent, which was the most
spoken of all the languages of the various races. He smoothly made
his way down a path he had used many times before, and when Dale
finally stopped, it was in front of the door to a certain shop.

Above the entrance was an ironwork sign with a strange ocelot
design on it, and there were flags lined up, all bearing the emblem
of a winged horse on green ground. This was the "Dancing Ocelot,"
both a bar and an inn. Dale passed by the entrance, went around to
the back of the building, and peeked into the kitchen from the rear.

"Kenneth, are you here?"

"Yeah. So you're back, huh, Dale?" said the big, unshaven man named Kenneth, who had been moving around a frying pan. He turned towards Dale and looked puzzled. "...Wait, what's that?"

"Well, I'll give you the details later, but... I just found her."

"Don't say it like you just picked up a dog or cat." Heartily arranging the finished food on a plate, Kenneth only looked more troubled upon hearing Dale's reply.

The large man was certainly good-natured, but not so long ago he was a capable adventurer who swung around a massive battle axe. That was a well-known fact amongst those who frequented this shop.

"For the time being, is it okay if we use the bath?"

"Well, I don't mind, but..."

Having received Kenneth's permission, Dale opened the door to the small hut next to the rear entrance, where the bath was. With a stone-tiled floor and a single bathtub, it was a simple bathing area, but it was plenty capable of fulfilling its function.

Dale poured his magic into the fire and water "magical device" to the side of the bathtub. While checking the temperature, he filled the tub with hot water.

The magical device not only provided water, but also made it easy to heat it. Even so, most households weren't equipped with baths. People generally used the public bathhouses throughout town instead.

The Dancing Ocelot had a bath out of consideration for the adventurers so they could bathe despite returning from work at all hours. After all, there were definitely a lot of them who returned in a horrible state, like Dale had been just a few hours earlier.

Latina watched Dale's actions intently, maybe finding even the magical device itself unusual.

Dale took off his coat and put it in the corner alongside his gauntlet, sword, and other belongings, and then called for Latina.

"Latina, 'come,'" he repeatedly beckoned, and the girl came to Dale's side.

When he tried to take off her clothes, Latina resisted Dale for the first time.

"Ah... So you really are a girl," Dale muttered while stripping the reluctant Latina naked and throwing her into the tub. He had already guessed that from her voice and clothes, but he hadn't been certain of it until just now.

The water washed over her hair and her painfully bony body, and it soon turned pitch black. Dale put soap into the tub, and it bubbled up right away. He washed Latina's greasy, dirty hair, which had become matted and rope-like. He washed her body as well, and once more replaced the dirty water.

As he filled the tub with bathwater and continued to wash Latina's hair, he suddenly realized something.

Huh? Could it be... that this girl will be a real beauty someday?

As he washed her hair over and over, it regained a platinum-like shine. Her single remaining horn also started to look like a glossy black gemstone.

Her ribcage was showing and she was painfully thin, but she would recover over time. Devils were a tenacious race by nature, after all. Her face was haggard as well, so up 'til now it was her eyes that primarily stood out, but once the grime was wiped off, it became clear that she possessed wonderful facial features as well. If her cheeks gained some plumpness and her complexion improved, then she'd make for quite an adorable young girl.

Agh, this only gives me an even more uneasy conscience and makes it harder to let her go...

25

If he let go of her hand, then some lecher would surely scoop her up right away. It was said that devils who lost a horn were abandoned by their own race, and had no one to support them. She'd be perfect prey for the sort that have inappropriate thoughts about young children.

I decided to get involved with her, so I need to prepare myself, thought Dale as he made that secret decision in the depths of his heart.

"So, you committed some sort of crime, Dale?" a young woman's voice called out to him from behind. When Dale looked, he saw a woman with black hair coming out of the back of the Dancing Ocelot. It was Kenneth's wife, Rita.

The Dancing Ocelot was an inn run by the young couple.

Rita was clearly startled at the sight of Dale vigorously washing a young girl. "Is that your illegitimate love child?"

"Where'd you get an idea like that? Just how old do you think I am?!" Dale shot back in disgust. "I picked her up in the forest. Her dad's corpse was there too," he added plainly.

As she listened, Rita took a long, hard look at the girl and realized her pitiful state and that she wasn't human. Then her eyes stopped on the worn-out cloth laying off to the side.

"Is that seriously what she was wearing? You don't intend to have her put that back on, right?"

"Ah, I forgot…"

"Hold on a minute."

Rita turned around and went back into the shop.

For the moment, Dale had just been thinking of getting her clean, but he hadn't even considered needing to get her a change of clothes.

"Dale, *****?"

"Hmm? 'Now, question'… Are you asking who that was just now? She's Rita, the proprietress of this place."

"…? Rita?"

"That's right, Rita."

As Latina tilted her head in confusion, Rita returned. She was holding a piece of cloth, along with all sorts of other items.

"Now that I look, you didn't even bring anything to dry her off with, did you?! Use this. And these are my old clothes, though I think they may be a little too big for her. Oh, and underwear!"

"Right, sorry about that. Thanks, Rita."

Dale looked hesitant as Rita tactlessly thrust a pair of underwear at him.

"What's with that expression? They're freshly sewn and brand new. It's not like I'd try to give you secondhand underwear to put on her," Rita said bluntly. That was the sort of woman Rita was. Perhaps she needed to be in order to run a shop that served adventurers.

Dale lifted Latina up out of the tub and wrapped her up in the soft cloth Rita had given him. While he was still drying her off, Latina pointed a finger at Rita.

"Dale, Rita?"

"Yeah, that's right."

"Rita, Latina." Latina then pointed at herself and gave Rita a quick bow.

"Oh wow, how impressive, introducing yourself like that!" Rita squatted down to Latina's eye level and smiled wide. The proprietress was fond of children by nature, and Dale knew that she and Kenneth were hoping to be blessed with a child soon.

"Rita, Latina only understands the devil language."

"Is that so? Then how have you been talking to her?"

"The words used in spells are the same, so I've been able to manage by picking out words that fit."

"Hmm. So, what are you planning on doing with her?"

"I was hoping to use the shop's Akhdar's Message Board to look into things, to start with."

Latina put on the clothes she was handed, without needing Dale's help. It seemed that she could at least manage that much by

29

herself. She was apparently more level-headed than she looked. She wouldn't have been able to survive in such a harsh environment otherwise, after all.

While Latina finished changing, Dale carried his baggage into the shop through the back entrance. As she didn't have a change of shoes, he picked her up again once she was done. Following Rita through the rear door, they passed through the kitchen and came into the front of the store.

There were a decent number of customers eating, so it was still moderately busy. The shop was naturally busiest before noon and after sunset. At the moment, Kenneth was still handling the shop by himself. Dale sat down at the corner of the counter and faced Rita.

"Now then, what did you want to look up?"

"Her name is Latina. A devil. Let's take a look with those terms. There may be a search out for her, after all."

"Right, we need to do that."

Rita gave a nod from the other side of the counter and slid her hand over the item known as "Akhdar's Message Board."

"Lawh, sajjal, yanadi."

The board glowed with pale green light in response. Though her eyes were pointed straight at the board, it seemed as though Rita was looking somewhere far, far away, searching for something distant.

"Hmm, there's not any information meeting those criteria. I'll try searching again using her physical traits as well just in case, but…"

"Please do."

The Akhdar's Message Board Rita was operating was the shop's greatest asset. Akhdar was the god who offered protection to travelers, who in turn controlled the flow of information. And so Akhdar's temples had become a place for the gathering and management of all sorts of intel and knowledge. The god's priests and ministers were able to use far more powerful data transmission magic than that of the normal populace, the primary reason being that they had the power of divine protection.

Thanks to this, the temples of Akhdar were able to share the same information even if they were in different regions, and some of that information was shared throughout the towns as well.

The points of contact for that transmission were places that flew flags with Akhdar's crest (a winged horse on green ground), the way that this shop had them up outside.

According to one theory, temple priests and ministers wanted to concentrate on gathering information and found it annoying to deal with people's requests for data, so they entrusted the whole process to outsiders. Because Akhdar priests were rather eccentric, this explanation had a ring of truth to it.

The information spread to the towns primarily concerned top news from around the world, new discoveries, and inventions. But what was given the greatest priority of all was news related to crimes.

People who committed serious crimes were considered "Wanted" the whole world over. But it was difficult for armies and government officials to cross national borders to pursue criminals, so they offered bounties through the temples in order to capture them. Among adventurers, there were certainly many who specialized in chasing after such rewards.

Requests for tasks like large-scale magical beast extermination were also delivered by the temples.

An Akhdar's Message Board acted as a terminal to receive information from the shrines, and in turn, adventurers seeking information were drawn to stores that possessed them; furthermore, townspeople also came to such places with requests for those adventurers. In addition to being a bar and inn, the Dancing Ocelot also served as a go-between for adventurers seeking work.

"Sure enough, there's nothing about her."

"Then Latina didn't commit a serious crime, after all. And if her parents aren't looking for her, then that corpse was definitely her father…"

Did Latina recognize that Dale and Rita's serious discussion was about her? She fidgeted about on Dale's lap, her gaze darting all over, and she occasionally looked up at the young adventurer.

The grim-looking men eating their meals occasionally glanced over their way as well, drawn by the unusual sight of a young child in this sort of shop. Whenever their eyes met, Latina tilted her head in confusion and stared right back at them.

As that was going on, a strange noise suddenly came from Latina. To be specific, her stomach was rumbling.

"…Latina?"

"Ah, the smell must have gotten to her."

Latina looked somewhat embarrassed to have both Dale and Rita watching her at the same time. Rita let out a hearty laugh and called out to Kenneth.

"Kenneth, make this kid some dinner. And make it something easy to digest, alright?"

"I'll take some too, if you don't mind," said Dale, and then he moved from the counter to a table. Since the table was too high for Latina, he had her sit on a small box on top of the chair to help boost her up, and then brought over his own chair and sat down next to her.

"So, what are you planning on doing with her, Dale?" asked Rita.

"I'll look after her. I mean, she can't speak our language, and she's from a different race, so even if I handed her over to an orphanage in a town that's always getting hit by budget deficits like this one, nothing good would come of it."

Saying that aloud was also partially to make up his mind to do it. It's not as though Dale was looking at the duty of raising a child lightly.

"I'm going to be this child's father."

†

Latina's grey eyes grew wide when a steaming hot plate of milk and cheese risotto was placed before her. Beside it was a soup made of smoked meat and finely diced vegetables. To the side of that compact arrangement of food was a mountain many times that size for Dale, with a large sausage heaped on his plate as well.

"Isn't Latina's serving a little small?"

"Don't be dumb. There's no way such a tiny girl could eat the same stupidly large amount that you do," Rita uttered in disgust after having served them. "And overeating like that would just destroy her stomach."

Rita then smiled wide as she handed Latina a spoon. The difference between this and how she treated Dale and the other customers was like night and day.

"Dale? ********?"

"Right, just eat."

Dale realized that this waif of a child was seeking his permission for each and every little thing. Even if he couldn't understand her words, he could tell that much just by looking at the expression on her face.

Latina was startled when she scooped up a spoonful of the risotto and placed it in her mouth. From how she hurriedly panted with her mouth wide open, it seemed the food was hotter than she'd expected.

"Rita, water!"

"Oh, was it too hot?"

Latina was blowing as hard as she could on the second spoonful. Dale laughed wildly at the sight, and Rita frowned a little.

Having blown on it for a while, Latina chomped down on the risotto, and her expression suddenly brightened. She was certainly easy to understand.

"I see, so it's tasty. That's great!" Dale took a bite of his portion, and his expression lit up as well. With Latina enjoying it so much right next to him, the food strangely seemed to taste better, even though it should've just been the same as always. To put it into words, Dale would say that he felt a sort of gentle aura coming from her.

Latina smiled and laughed. It was the first time he'd seen her smile.

"Right, just keep on eating, Latina. Do you want some sausage, too?"

"I told you, you shouldn't overfeed her!"

Having carried out water, Rita saw Dale trying to heap plenty of food onto Latina's plate from his own, so she smacked him with the tray. Latina looked shocked.

"But she needs her nutrients, right?!"

"Yeah, but I'm saying that she shouldn't shovel it all in at once! Kenneth and I are going to make some child-sized, between-meal snacks! It'll be less food at once, but a greater number of meals!"

A far-off voice seemed to say, "*I'm the one who's gonna make it, but whatever...*" but neither of them paid it any attention. All the while, Latina kept on eating in tiny bites, so despite how much more he had on his plate, Dale finished eating first.

And then, as if she had been timing out when Latina would finish eating, Rita brought out another plate; this one held a few pieces of fruit compote. The shop didn't usually have sweets on its menu, making this the first time such a desert was served there.

"You'd never guess from looking at him that Kenneth has a soft spot for children…"

The food was still slightly warm, so it was likely created off the cuff especially for Latina.

When it was set down in front of her, the girl once more looked at Dale for approval, and when she saw him nod, she put the fruit in her mouth. Her expression lit up more than ever before; her eyes were absolutely sparkling.

"It's good, huh?"

Seeing as she ate it in a daze, it seemed clear that Latina was quite fond of the compote. It must've been all she could manage just to find something edible in that forest. There's no way she would've eaten anything so sweet there.

"How about it? Is it yummy?"

Having finished carrying food to the other customers, Rita stared at Latina and received an even greater smile than before in response. It was so wide a smile that it seemed like flowers in full bloom would burst out behind her. Even if they couldn't exchange words, it was a more than sufficient response.

I need to hurry up and teach her the language so she won't end up getting lured away with food by some weirdo… Seeing Latina's smile, Dale gripped his fists tightly under the table, realizing that he was buying her favor with food as well.

After finishing eating, Latina stared at the plate where the compote had once been.

And so, Dale stroked Latina's hair. Perhaps surprised by the suddenness of it, she sprung right up. But when she saw the expression on his face, her tension melted away.

"Did I startle you? Sorry about that. You're tired out from today, right? All sorts of stuff happened, after all."

Although Latina tilted her head a little as she listened to him, she kept her eyes on him the entire time, as if she was trying to decipher his intentions. When Dale thought about it, the girl was paying careful attention to her surroundings. Maybe she had an acute sense of observation, but perhaps in exchange she was too trustful.

Dale picked Latina up, and she placed her arms around his neck on her own. It was awkward, since she was still trying to rely on him, but her clinging to him helped keep his balance nice and stable. Supporting Latina with one arm, Dale headed towards the counter once more.

"Rita, I want to let Latina rest, so I'm heading for my room."

"Got it. Good night, Latina."

Hearing Rita's voice, Latina gave another wide smile. Even in this short amount of time, she seemed to have come to recognize Dale and Rita as people it was safe to be around. Since meeting them, her expression had grown noticeably gentler.

The warm, fuzzy feeling it gave Dale was almost embarrassing.

Dale had changed quite a bit as well in the brief time since they met. Even yesterday, he never would have thought that he could feel this way about a kid.

Dale went past the counter and through the kitchen. Seeing the back of Kenneth as he struggled at his work, he called out, "Kenneth, Latina says the fruit was tasty."

"Right!" Kenneth responded without turning around as Dale passed behind him and towards the stairs in back, where ingredients were piled up.

He cut straight across the second floor and climbed a ladder, arriving in the attic.

Since it was used to stockpile miscellaneous goods to be sold to the adventurers down on the first floor, there was baggage strewn all about; but even further in was a corner that showed signs of being lived in. That was the corner Dale was renting.

Having a place to live was also one of the reasons that he was able to decide to take Latina in. Dale wasn't a citizen of the town, but because he'd been working from here for quite a while and it was inconvenient to move around from inn to inn, he'd ended up relying on his old friend, Kenneth, and renting this place.

It became an easy decision to rent the attic when Rita, who had been using it as her own room, married Kenneth. As long as you could ignore the somewhat low ceiling, it was a plenty fine dwelling.

Dale also had no problem paying and wouldn't do anything as pathetic and stingy as pilfering from the inventory or luggage, so it seemed he wasn't such a bad tenant for the owners, either, since they knew his personality and lifestyle.

Dale let Latina down in his "room." There was a carpet with a foreign feel to it spread out on the floor, and near the window was a desk and shelf. Other than that, there was a bed and a large, lidded box. It was a small amount of belongings for a town resident, but a large amount for a traveler.

"'Little, wait, this place.'" Seeing Latina nod her head, Dale went back down to grab his coat and other belongings he'd left behind.

While waiting for him to return, Latina wandered about the room. It seemed the girl was indeed quite inquisitive. She also had a strong sense of self-restraint, as she only looked at things rather than touching them. It was difficult to remember back to when he was that age, but when he thought about the children always playing about town, Dale realized that she really was level-headed for a kid.

Dale kicked off his boots and entered his own territory. In the culture where he was born, you sat directly on the floor rather than on chairs, and he at least wanted his own room to have a comfortable, intimate style to it. That was also why he had a rug with the feel of his old home spread out, and he didn't want to dirty it.

He hung his coat up next to the box, then placed down his luggage. His weapons went on top of the shelf near his bed, as they usually did. Dale opened the window and let in fresh air, then took off his stab-resistant tunic as well as his heavy pants.

"Come here, Latina."

Picking up on the meaning from his beckoning hand gesture, Latina obediently came closer. Dale then got into the bed, bringing her along with him. Compared to his normal routine, it was still pretty early to go to bed, but an adventurer's ability to rest when they needed to was an indispensable skill, so it was no trouble for him to sleep now.

He was worried about what he was going to do if Latina didn't like this, but she obediently snuggled down next to him and curled up like a kitten. It wasn't long until she nodded off.

She really was tired. She still drifted off, even though she's surrounded by people she doesn't know and doesn't understand our language or what's going on.

Dale stroked Latina's hair and felt so calm that he even surprised himself. It was strange that he felt this way, even though he had only just decided to become her parent.

It may not be so bad to live together with someone else like this, Dale thought, falling asleep while feeling a warmer body next to his own.

Before long, Latina woke Dale up with a barrage of tiny blows, her face as white as a sheet.

The word that Latina ended up asking to learn first was "bathroom."

And incidentally, Latina was able to maintain her dignity.

Dale woke up fairly early the next morning. He'd gone to bed early the night before, after all. Casting his eyes toward the other presence he felt in his bed, he noticed the girl lying next to him.

"Oh, that's right. I brought her back with me from the forest…" he muttered, remembering his new roommate as he let out a yawn.

Latina held tightly onto a bit of Dale's clothing as she breathed, somewhat out of tune, in her sleep. Dale pondered how he could get out of bed without waking her, but her eyes shot open the second he sat up. She jumped up as if in a panic, hot on Dale's heels.

Sensing her anxiety, Dale shot her a smile, trying to calm her down at least a little. "Good morning, Latina," he said as he patted her head.

Dale got out of bed and changed into a simple shirt and comfortable pants, different from the clothes that he wore for work. With only a coin purse and a knife on his waist, he ran his fingers through his bed head to get it under control. Finally, he slipped on his boots and scooped Latina up. She didn't have a single change of clothes, so she was still wearing what she had on when she went to sleep, and her skirt had gotten a little wrinkled.

Dale went down to the first floor and took Latina towards a table in the kitchen, rather than into the store itself.

"Oh, my. Good morning, Latina." Rita smiled, noticing the two. That smile, of course, was only directed at the young girl.

Kenneth and Rita were right in the middle of making breakfast. Adventurers tended to eat a lot, even early in the morning, so the couple needed a lot more food than what was required for just the lodgers. On top of all that, there were also customers who only came to eat breakfast. While it was great for business, it was also an impossibly busy time for the shop owners.

Dale kept going around the back and washed his face at the sink by the bathing area. He cleaned off the hand towel he'd used and handed it to Latina while it was still dripping wet. Apparently, Latina properly grasped what he meant, as she wiped her own face clean with it.

After he washed his undergarments as well, Dale's usual morning routine was complete. He finished by hanging them up in the nearby area set aside for drying. As he headed back inside, he found Rita combing Latina's hair. All the while, Rita's expression was full of awe and admiration, as well as restlessness.

"Latina's hair is a beautiful color. It really is wonderful. Hey, Dale, you moron, you can't leave a girl's hair all messy the way you do with yours!"

It was definitely true that Latina's hair was far shinier than it had been before having a comb passed through it. The new father made a mental note.

Rita skillfully gathered up Latina's hair and tied it with ribbons. Together, her hair and the ribbons almost completely hid Latina's horns.

"Putting aside the fact that she's a devil, it'd at least be a good idea to make sure that her one broken horn doesn't stand out," whispered Rita while shooting Dale a sideways glance.

"Got it, thanks," he replied, and his gaze fell on Latina.

There were no changes to her physique, but having been cleaned up, her hair done, and dressed in proper clothes, Latina clearly looked like a cute little girl. Compared to the filthy child that he'd found in the forest, whose gender he hadn't even been able to determine, she was like a completely different person.

"Hey, good morning! Here's your breakfast." Passing by Rita, Kenneth appeared with plates in both hands.

Latina faced Kenneth, and after thinking a little, she said, "Good murnnin." She didn't seem to have much confidence in how she'd done, as she quickly lowered her head.

Kenneth froze as the expression on Dale's face distorted. Latina seemed to have figured out that it was a greeting after having heard the same words said to her all morning. The girl really did seem to have an acute sense of observation. Dale had a vague feeling that she may be rather clever as well.

"***? *****?"

"No, that was right. 'Correct.'" Dale let out a hurried laugh, realizing that the expression on his face had made Latina worry that she had used it incorrectly. "Damn it, I'll get back at you for this, Kenneth." Even so, Dale kept a smile on his face as he complained to Kenneth, who had stolen away Latina's "first greeting."

"Don't be so childish." Kenneth's expression lightened up a bit as well. "Rita and I really should have one of our own soon." Murmuring about how great children were, Kenneth returned to his work station.

Dale's breakfast was a normal grilled cheese and smoked meat sandwich, but Latina's portion was custom-made. The bread had been dipped in milk and egg and cooked until the inside became all creamy, and then the compote from yesterday was place on top. The smoked meat had been thinly chopped and then fried until crispy so it could be used as a garnish. And in addition to all that, the glass in front of Latina was filled with chilled fruit juice.

What had cooled it down was a "magical device," which was the general term for tools that made use of the power known as "magic" that existed inside all people. Lately, these devices had become common among the general populace. Visit any home, and you'd most likely find magical devices for "Water," "Fire," and "Water/Dark," which were all for use in the kitchen. In other words, they were used to supply drinking water, light a fire, and refrigerate with ice, respectively. Magical devices obviously cost a good bit of money, so there were of course those who used the communal well, or lit their fires with a chimney starter. But because convenience couldn't be beat, those people were overwhelmingly in the minority. As a result, frozen foods weren't exactly uncommon these days.

Latina gulped down the fruit juice and turned to face Dale, looking overjoyed.

"Ah, great. …That bastard Kenneth really is trying to win her over with food." Dale muttered the last part quietly so Latina couldn't hear.

Latina was completely absorbed in devouring the bread as well. It seemed she was really fond of sweets.

"Hey Rita, where can I go to buy little girls' clothes and stuff like that?" asked Dale as he carried over his plate, having finished eating. When he saw Latina, who was only halfway through her meal, staring at him and looking flustered, Dale sat down where she could see him. Thanks to his strong sense of duty, which made him feel the need to help out when someone was busy with something, he started peeling the skins off of a mountain of potatoes. "Also, could you tell me anything else that I need to get right away? Like, things that'd be easy for a guy like me to overlook."

"Let's see… If you want a tailor, then Amanda's shop in the eastern district has a good reputation, and well, the weather's good, so the market should be outside in the plaza, too—it may not be a bad idea to look for secondhand clothes there as well. Go to Bart's place for the shoes. It's the shop on the corner. And then…" Rita stopped working and grabbed a pen so she could make a list.

Hearing all this, Dale grasped just a fragment of how determined women were when it came to shopping, and he trembled.

After a short bit of waiting for Latina to finish eating, Dale scooped the girl up and left the Dancing Ocelot.

"First up is shoes… Can't have you walking around barefoot, after all."

Her weight itself wasn't any trouble, but he'd need to carry bags as well.

"Dale?"

"'Shopping' is, how should I put it…?" Dale talked to himself and wondered if he should buy her a picture book or something. This wouldn't be a cheap shopping trip, but it wasn't enough that it'd be a serious strain on him, either.

As they approached the center of town, the sight of adventurers became less frequent, while the number of residents increased. At the market held in the plaza in the center, there were both people from neighboring villages and traveling merchants selling their wares. There were many who came here to sell what they had.

Dale turned off onto a side street halfway across the plaza and headed towards the eastern district. Just as Rita instructed, he entered the shop belonging to the craftsman named Bart.

A few hours later, Dale was completely exhausted and slumped on a seat in the plaza.

"I-I'm wiped…" he muttered, his head hung low in exhaustion. Next to him was a mountain of large bags.

To be perfectly honest, cutting down magical beasts was easier than this. He hadn't imagined that it would be so torturous to keep going into stores filled only with women and buying things he wasn't used to purchasing. He'd really wanted to call it quits when faced with stares as he held little girls' underwear in his hands. If Latina hadn't been by his side, then someone really might have ended up calling the town guard on him.

Dale was plagued by such pessimistic thoughts as he suffered from exhaustion.

"Dale, *******?"

"Yeah, you don't need to worry. 'Negate, problem'… It's alright."

"All, right?"

"Yeah, you got it."

Latina was seated by his side and eating a piece of fruit he had bought for her in the market. Before he left, Rita told him over and over to make sure that she stayed hydrated and fed.

Once she finished eating the juicy pieces Dale had cut up for her, Latina looked down at her now sticky hands and became lost in thought. After staring at them for a while, Latina looked up at Dale, seemingly at a loss.

"You may have actually had a pretty good upbringing, Latina…"

The brats prowling around here would've probably long since wiped their hands off on their sleeves. Having watched Latina since yesterday, he'd gotten the impression that she was very well-mannered.

Of course, there was also the fact that she was still nervous around Dale. It seemed this clever young girl was still concerned about things like that.

"Oh water, heed my call, and appear. 《Appear: Water》" The ball of water summoned by Dale's short chant burst over Latina's hands. "Now to dry her hands... I should buy plenty of handkerchiefs for Latina as well, huh...?" mumbled Dale, standing up and looking out over market once more, not yet realizing that in heading back in, he'd end up buying far more than what he had initially planned. He'd only become aware of this when he returned holding a mountain of bags and saw Rita and Kenneth's faces.

It wasn't long before he had gathered up all the things he needed to buy, but that was about the time that Latina started to look rather tired.

"Are you alright, Latina?"

But when Dale asked that, she responded by saying, "Alright," and nodding. It may have been a mistake to teach that word to such a considerate child. He let out a single sigh and shuffled the luggage so he could pick Latina up.

"Dale, alright."

"'Fatigue, heal, overdo, negate.'"

When Latina shook her head even to that, Dale admonished her with a pat on the back. Even the bulky luggage and Latina together weren't too much for him to carry.

Just as Dale had expected, by the time he reached the Dancing Ocelot, Latina had fallen asleep in his arms.

As always, Latina's breathing as she slept was somewhat out of tune. Even now, Dale could hear a "*kuh-pyoo*" sound emanating from her tiny body.

Latina continued her nap on top of an impromptu bed made by lining up a few chairs. There were hardly any customers in the Dancing Ocelot at the moment. It was still too early for dinner, but

47

it was also too late to look for work. There were only travelers and adventurers seeking information here and there about the shop.

Dale was drinking watered-down wine while watching over Latina as she slept. He let out a moan.

"What's with that depressing face?" asked Rita as she manned the shop from the other side of the counter. She looked surprised.

"It's that job from yesterday. I have to report that I finished it, but... with the way things were, I couldn't exactly cut off anything to bring it back."

"Ah, that. They really smelled, right? If you tried to bring anything back, you wouldn't have been allowed through the gate."

"If you knew that, then you should've told me."

"If I did that, then nobody would've taken the job, right?" Rita replied, as if that was only natural.

And with that, he realized why the conditions for completing the job were set up the way that they were.

"I've gotta take the client along to check the site. I'll probably be back late tomorrow."

The client for this job was listed under a joint signature of doctors from around Kreuz. Apparently, the magical beasts had constructed their colony right in the only place in the region that a certain medicinal plant grew. According to the contract, he needed to bring a doctor to the site the following day in order to prove that he had exterminated the magical beasts.

For jobs like this, normally you would carve off part of the magical beast, such as an ear, and bring it back with you. But the "frogs" this time had been an exception. There weren't many magical beasts that gave off such a horrible stench.

Having finished the job, now he needed to set aside time to help confirm it. He couldn't make the client wait, but he couldn't bring

Latina along either—that area was inhabited by magical beasts. He was worried about being separated from the girl he had just taken under his wing, but it would just be too dangerous to bring her along. But would it really be alright to leave such a young girl all alone?

"How about just leaving her here?" said Rita, easily cutting right through Dale's worries. "I'll add the babysitting fee to this month's rent."

"…Is that really alright?"

"You have no other choice, right? But it's just this once, okay? Next time, you need to look for a babysitter yourself."

And so, Dale's next problem became how to tell Latina about all of this.

The first thing Latina said after waking from her nap was, "Dale?" in a voice that sounded like she was about to cry. This was more than her new father felt he deserved. When she heard him reply, "I'm right here," she was clearly relieved. She got down from the chairs and came to Dale's side as he was writing up documents at the counter. As her tiny hands grasped Dale's clothes tightly and she looked up at him, the worried look on his face evaporated.

"This is bad, Rita. I can't just leave Latina all alone without me!"

"Don't be stupid. It's dangerous, right?!"

"It's fine. I'll protect Latina, even if I have to abandon the client."

Rita had "This guy may be hopeless after all" written all over her face.

"Dale?"

"Latina… Gah, I really hate this! Maybe I could choose Latina over the reward money…"

"You idiot. You're going to have to travel far away for your usual "work" soon enough anyway, right? If you don't have the backbone to leave her home at this point, then it'll be impossible for you to raise her at all."

Rita's argument was sound. His work was dangerous, and it wasn't the sort of thing where you could bring a child along. One way or another, there'd be plenty of times where she'd have to stay behind. Rita and Kenneth were here, so there'd be no worries about her getting fed. And it should be far safer and more pleasant for her here than it was when she was living alone in the forest. It'd be fine, surely.

But whether or not he could accept that was a different matter altogether. He should've known from the start that there were going to be times that he'd make Latina feel lonely, but...

"Ugh..."

If he said that he didn't want to leave Latina alone at this point, there was no way Dale could ever give her over to an orphanage.

This was something that he absolutely needed to overcome. It had just come sooner than he had expected. He understood that.

"What... a cruel trial..." Dale muttered without thinking. Now "Ah, he really is hopeless" was written on Rita's face.

In the end, Latina obediently heard him out. With a serious look on her face, she quietly and intently listened to Dale's clumsy words, and with a firm frown, as if she were swallowing down the emotions welling up inside her, she seemed to decide to bear it.

"Alright," she replied, along with a nod.

Deep down, the adults who saw this all thought, *So innocent. This girl is just too innocent...*

The one with the most striking reaction of all was Dale, who was starting to lose sight of the man he had been before yesterday.

"I'm sorry! I'm so sorry, Latina!" Without even thinking about it, he grasped her tight in a hug. Latina looked surprised.

"Dale? Latina, alright." In a way, her saying that made her much more of an adult than Dale.

She didn't need to grow up so fast, though.

Now absolutely brimming with the desire to pamper her, Dale lifted Latina up and carried her to their room. The room was currently packed full of the things that he had bought earlier. Dale had carried them all in while Latina was sleeping.

In front of the young girl, he tidied up everything that he had purchased. The reason he did this, while saying what each thing was as he put it away, was to teach her words.

Her clothes and underwear went into a big hamper, and he put the accessories into a smaller basket. He lined these up where the slope of the roof had created something of a dead space, thinking that even a tiny girl like Latina could reach them there. He had bought a great number of picture books as well, so he lined those up on the bottom of the shelf.

Latina watched closely as Dale cleaned up. She seemed to realize that Dale had bought all of these things for her.

Having finished straightening up, Dale had Latina sit on his lap and opened up one of the picture books he had purchased. It was a book meant to teach young children letters. The premium-priced book had colored illustrations with names written beside them, but the contents were extraordinarily simple. Looking at Latina, he figured that the contents were far too easy for her, but he had purchased it so it could serve as a textbook to teach her words and letters.

Dale slowly read through the book aloud. As though not even wanting to spare a single blink, Latina leaned forward and concentrated full-force on the pages. Sure enough, her reaction was far more grown-up than her age would imply.

Every once in a while, she'd point at the book and ask a question. "Dale, **, *****?"

"Hmm? Yeah, that's right."

Once he'd finished reading through it he looked over at Latina; she seemed to have understood the purpose of the book. She opened it back up to the first page and looked up at Dale pressingly. As he read through it again, pausing after each word, she repeated each one back, mimicking him.

"Dog, cat, horse."

"Doog, cait, hurse." She was just too cute as she mispronounced the words with an overly serious expression on her face, and so he was unable to correct her.

He continued to gaze lovingly at Latina as she remained absorbed in the picture book, only realizing how much time had passed when he saw the sun setting through the window. And so he decided to take Latina to the bath before the sun went down completely. Being a new father, Dale didn't know what sort of illnesses children could catch, but he decided it'd be best to keep her clean.

He was still anxious about the idea of taking her to a bathhouse, so for the time being he decided he would use the Dancing Ocelot's bath. In exchange, he was ordered to help clean up.

"No matter how levelheaded she may be, you absolutely *can't* leave children all alone in the bath! There've been plenty of accidents where kids ended up drowning like that!" scolded Rita.

Even so, Latina looked reluctant today as well when Dale took her clothes off. For now, at least, this was the only time that the girl would pout at him. It didn't seem like she hated bathing itself, but there was definitely something about the whole process that she wasn't fond of. Dale wondered about that as he watched Latina play about and scoop up bubbles in her hands.

After finishing the bath and having dinner, Dale scooped up Latina, who was nodding off again, and returned to their room to put her in bed. Remembering what had happened the day before, he also made sure she went to the bathroom first.

"…Goodnight, Latina," whispered Dale as he stroked her hair.

Half asleep at this point, Latina responded with a "G'night… Dale." Dale had to hold back the urge to squeeze her tightly, or else he'd wake her up.

He spent the night feeling her gentle warmth cradled in his arms, until the break of dawn.

Dale never thought he would find the arrival of morning so terribly painful. When she saw Dale stricken by such grief, Rita was completely exasperated.

"Just give it up and get going already."

"Latina, I'll be back as soon as I possibly can. Be a good girl," said Dale as he hugged Latina, who was standing in front of the Dancing Ocelot beside Rita. Even though he knew that most of his words wouldn't get through to her, he still needed to say them.

Dale reluctantly let go when he felt the bloodlust emanating from Rita; she was going to kick him out if this went on any longer. Dale patted Latina on the head while looking straight at her and said, "I'm off."

Latina tilted her head in confusion.

"Tell him 'take care,' Latina," Rita said. Hearing her own name, Latina looked at Rita. "Take care."

Upon hearing Rita say it again, Latina faced Dale and awkwardly tried to repeat it.

"Dale, tak care?"

"Right, I'm off."

Seeing Dale's wide grin, Latina broke out in a smile as well.

†

The Dancing Ocelot was terribly busy in the morning.

Alongside the adventurers that were lodging here eating their meals, there were also those who had come to check the fliers for newly posted jobs. It would still be a while longer until most townsfolk would come in with jobs, but it's not as if there weren't people who came there early because they wanted things taken care of today, and it was necessary to deal with such clients as well. There were also adventurers heading out to work at this time, and they tended to purchase goods.

It was so busy that Rita and Kenneth could take any help that they could get.

Kenneth was darting about the bar, which at this time of day was serving more as a restaurant. Rita came out onto the floor now and again as well, but her primary focus was dealing with the Akhdar's Message Board and squaring up accounts. All the while, Latina watched the hectic goings-on in the shop with great interest.

"Oops, careful there!" called out Kenneth in surprise when he noticed Latina underfoot as he held two plates in each hand.

Latina tilted her head in confusion.

Today she was wearing a pink dress that Dale had bought for her just yesterday. Rita had helped her put her hair up, and it was swaying along with the big pink ribbons on each side of her head. Dale had also enthusiastically bought her plenty of hair ornaments, so she now had so many that she could change them out each day of the week.

Latina's eyes were locked on Kenneth as he carried out food, picked up the empty plates, and took orders. As Rita was spending most of her time on the other side of the counter and the girl couldn't understand what she was saying, Latina hadn't the slightest clue what she was doing. On the other hand, Kenneth's actions were easy to understand.

Up until now, Latina had intently watched Kenneth as he cooked, and now he was serving up a mountain of food so large that it was hard to tell how many portions it contained.

Nodding her head once, Latina toddled into the hustle and bustle of the shop.

"Hmm…?"

Kenneth first noticed something was strange when he turned around to face his work station to arrange the freshly finished scrambled eggs with smoked meat next to the mashed potatoes on a large plate. The number of plates had increased.

The size of the pile of dirty plates stacked next to the sink was growing. At first, he figured it was Rita bringing them in. This was a busy time for her too, but she occasionally got a free moment. But when Kenneth brought the completed food out into the shop, he saw Rita interacting with clients, selling miscellaneous goods, and even settling accounts with customers who'd come to eat. Under those circumstances, it'd be absolutely impossible for her to head out onto the floor.

"Sorry for the wait," he said as he set down the food in front of a familiar, bearded man. He was an adventurer who was an old regular, and his mouth was hanging wide open. "What's with that stupid look on your face?" Kenneth asked.

"You're one to talk. That's one hell of a tiny waitress you hired."

Looking in the direction that the regular was pointing, Kenneth at last realized what was going on.

Latina was walking with a plate in her hands. She was so tiny that a single plate was apparently all the weight she could manage to hold. She was heading for the kitchen and grasping it firmly in both hands.

After a short while, she returned to the shop and looked around. When she found an empty plate, she gave a single, satisfied nod and headed towards the table with a determined look on her face. Latina smiled at the customer, who was startled upon seeing the tiny girl, and then took hold of the empty dish. As she stumbled slightly, even customers other than the one at that table watched her anxiously. When she made it back to the kitchen safely, the intimidating-looking men all breathed a sigh of relief.

"Latina?" As Kenneth called out to her, Latina came to a halt and looked up at him worriedly. "Did I screw up?" was written all over her face.

Kenneth stopped and thought for a few moments.

Latina was properly paying attention to the customers before picking up the empty plates. She wasn't overestimating her own abilities; she was only doing what she was able to handle. She was mindful of her surroundings and avoided people nearby.

At any rate, she was able to maneuver without getting in the way, which meant that she paid heed to how she was moving about. That was proof that Latina was attentive of her surroundings.

Kenneth looked at the girl so tiny that her entire head could fit in his hand, and he ruffled her hair.

"Okay. It's fine, then." As he stroked her hair, Latina's head swayed about in Kenneth's hand, and she looked a little dizzy.

Even if he just left her alone, no harm would come of it, he decided. In fact, in some ways it might be nice to have a little help cleaning up. He realized that it might be a bit bad for the customers' hearts, though.

After the peak morning hours had passed, Kenneth got out a bowl he had prepared the night before from the "refrigerator."

"Latina."

She obediently came over when he called, and he sat her down at the kitchen table. Before she could see what was in the bowl, he turned it over and the contents slid out and wiggled all about. Latina's eyes opened wide.

Kenneth had chopped up what had remained of the compote and placed it in gelatin for today's afternoon snack. He handed Latina a spoon.

While doing the dishes, Kenneth looked over at Latina and saw how happy she looked as the gelatin jiggled about on the tip of the utensil.

Around noon, the flow of customers into the Dancing Ocelot came to a halt. That was when their primary customers, adventurers, headed out for work, so they temporarily closed the bar. During this time of day, they only accepted work involving the Akhdar's Message Board.

"Rita, I'm going to go replenish our stock," Kenneth called out into the shop.

Rita's response was politer than usual. "Take care."

Before he even had time to question it, a smile and a, "Tak care" came from Latina, who had docilely laid her picture book out on a corner of the counter.

"Children really are great, aren't they, Rita? Does three sound about right to you?"

"Let's just start with one before we get carried away."

Rita thought that he really was an idiot, but the look on Rita's face wasn't an entirely dissatisfied one.

Latina pattered up to Kenneth when he got back from stocking. Behind her, Rita was watching with a smirk on her face.

"Welcom bak." Latina turned back around to look at Rita, as if asking, "Did I do it right?"

"…"

Kenneth had purchased all sorts of fruit that he didn't usually buy when restocking, and they were soon rolling about his work station. As he rolled up his sleeves and wondered what he should make, he wore a goofy grin on his face. He had no room to talk when it came to Dale.

At any rate, Latina really was a well-mannered child.

When he brought her out a small cheese sandwich for lunch, she properly chewed as she ate, and once she was done, she took the empty plate to the sink herself. And at other times as well, she just looked through a picture book on her own, or watched Rita and Kenneth. It seemed she absolutely wouldn't make a hindrance of herself, and was always making sure that it was alright for her to be where she was.

According to Dale, she had survived in a place where magical beasts lived, and she had to search for her own food. While the experience was far too cruel for such a young child, it could also be said that it required an incredibly strong will and a lot of luck. But regardless, he had no idea how long she had done it.

Judging by her terribly thin body, if Dale hadn't found her, it wouldn't have been much longer before she would've wasted away and ended up in the belly of some beast. Perhaps that was why she seemed to be so hypersensitive about her surroundings.

As Kenneth watched, Latina started to nod off, and she staggered towards the stairs. Even if she was heading back to her room, letting her go up into the attic on her own when she was like that would be dangerous.

Kenneth saw some wooden boxes in the corner of the pantry next to the kitchen and put them side by side. He passed by Latina, who was still tottering along, and headed for his room on the second floor. He grabbed a mat and some sheets, then spread them on top of the boxes to complete the impromptu bed for her nap.

"Latina," he called, and gave the bed a tap to point it out to her. She was still at the bottom of the stairs, struggling to climb them while fighting off sleep. As she turned around, her eyes were already half-closed.

With a wry smile on his face, Kenneth lifted her up and tucked her in on top of the wooden boxes. She must've been right at her limit, as he started to hear the sound of her deeply breathing in her sleep in no time at all.

†

Latina's eyes shot open with a snap and darted around.

"Dale?" She called out the name of the person who had taken her out of that forest.

The person who found her when she was all on her own.

The person who gave her a safe place to live and food to eat.

The person who made her remember the warmth of other people.

She called out the name of the person who, to her, was a symbol that it was alright to relax.

"Are you up, Latina?"

Hearing the voice of a man other than Dale, Latina panicked. She felt like she needed to run away this very moment, and she put all of her strength into doing so.

But it was then that she recognized the sweet scent gently wafting through the air. With a quick blink of her eyes, Latina remembered where she was.

†

The first sound out of Latina when she woke from her nap was her calling out for Dale. That's what made Kenneth realize she was up.

Stirring a small pot, he checked on her and found her looking around like a frightened little animal on high alert. When Kenneth called her name, she only seemed to get more on edge. But rather than moving immediately, she saved her strength so she could act after she understood the situation.

Kenneth couldn't help but admire how sharp the girl was. Compared to those hot-blooded folks who called themselves novice adventurers, her judgment was much calmer and more precise. Considering her young age, it was no surprise that there was no helping the way that she lost sight of her situation after waking up from her nap.

Kenneth took the pot off of the fire and headed towards Latina.

As the berries broke down perfectly, a thick, sweet smell drifted through the air. Just as Kenneth had planned, as soon as Latina picked up the smell, the tension drained from her body.

After hopping down from the boxes, she toddled on over to Kenneth's side. As Latina peered into the pot held out before her, there wasn't a hint of that sense of a small animal bristling that he felt before. The look on her face now was absolutely appropriate for a young girl her age.

Having captured Latina's attention, Kenneth spread the freshly made jam over a thinly cut slice of bread. He wanted to slather it on, but if he did she'd ended up burning her mouth. He measured out an amount that would be plenty to provide a taste while also cooling quickly.

He handed it to Latina, and she looked up at him as if seeking approval. Timidly, she took a bite of the bread, and her expression instantly brightened.

While Latina was absorbed in eating it, the jam started to run like syrup. She licked the palm of her hand, which had stopped the flow, and then looked up at Kenneth suddenly. He was grinning rather than rebuking her, so Latina smiled right back.

For a while, Latina continued to stare without tiring at the jar Kenneth put the jam into. Kenneth truly felt the effort he had gone through to make it was worth it.

As the sun started to set, the adventurers gradually returned to town. That's when the Dancing Ocelot became busy again.

It's not as if all the customers who came to the Ocelot were lodgers. In fact, there were far more who came for the food and drink. In addition to the adventurers, there were also gatekeepers and town guards who were returning from work. Because it was a shop that didn't put on airs, where you could get cheap food and drink, it was a place where intimidating bastards tended to gather.

Once it got this late, they stopped taking work involving the Akhdar's Message Board. Rita instead shifted to working the floor, and so the couple managed to pull through the great hustle and bustle.

Latina, who was eating her dinner at a seat at the corner of the counter, had her attention stolen away by the liveliness of the shop as well. When she saw one of the customers let out a hearty laugh, the gnocchi she was carrying to her mouth fell with a plop. She didn't even realize it. Latina started observing the customer intently, her eyes wide. Kenneth thought she looked like she had encountered some new sort of creature for the first time, but he decided not to say that aloud.

Around when Latina's eyelids started to grow heavy, the door to the Dancing Ocelot opened.

"Oh, it's Dale."

Latina's eyes shot wide open when she heard Rita say that. She hopped down from the chair and hurriedly ran to meet him.

"Latina, I'm b—" Dale tried to say, only for her to tightly hug his legs. "Latina…"

As he frowned, figuring that he had indeed made Latina feel lonely, the young girl looked up at him and said, "Welcoom bak."

He froze halfway through bending over to pick her up.

Rita and Kenneth smirked. Unable to hold himself back from breaking out in a smile, Dale resumed his prior action and lifted Latina up.

"I'm back, Latina. You did a great job holding down the fort."

That made her grin grow even wider, and she was all smiles.

The regulars in the shop all knew Dale, so when they saw the doofy look on his face, they mercilessly teased him.

"Geez, Dale, that's an awful tiny girlfriend you've got there."

"Oh, shut up!" While fending off this cruel treatment, Dale took a seat, still holding Latina in his arms. Seeing Rita carrying out food, Dale asked, "Has Latina had dinner?"

"She ate a while ago. In fact, she was just getting sleepy before you came in."

The girl in question was sitting on Dale's lap, a satisfied and relieved-looking smile on her face. It was such a lovely sight that those looking at her felt their hearts melt.

"So, how was it? Did Latina behave herself?"

"She was almost *too* well-behaved. This kid is incredibly clever. She properly understands the situation she's in and knows what sort of action she should take," said Rita as she sloppily filled the goblet in front of Dale with wine.

As far as alcohol went, Dale only ever drank wines that had a low alcoholic content. Knowing this, Rita picked a wine for him without even asking. It was well known in the shop that it wasn't because he *couldn't* drink or didn't like to, but because he hated being dead drunk. A regular had called him childish when he was a first-time customer, leading to the incident of "Dale easily beating a regular with one arm behind his back," which had become a beloved drinking topic in the shop.

Latina rubbed her cheek up against Dale's chest like a pampered kitten. Whenever their eyes met, a joyous smile popped onto her face. This may have been the most that she'd ever been pampered.

Rather than making me feel guilty, this may have actually been a bit of a good thing...

He cherished this little girl so much that he thought perhaps it wouldn't be so bad leaving her behind, if it'd make her want to be spoiled so badly.

†

It wasn't even a week before definitive proof that Latina was extremely clever appeared.

Latina had become able to handle everyday conversations with seemingly little difficulty. That was when Dale was assailed by a certain worry: Latina had become attached to Kenneth. Dale didn't even try to hide the grumpy displeasure on his face as he watched Latina chase after the shopkeeper like a chick following after its parent.

Over her dress, Latina was wearing an apron that Dale didn't recall buying; she also had on a bandana made from the same material. It was the look of a little child acting as a "helper."

Latina was giving her all to wiping off the tables beside Kenneth as he cleaned the shop.

They... look like a father and daughter when she's next to Kenneth like that...

Dale had been worried about him to begin with.

Kenneth's been luring Latina in through her stomach from the very start!

More than worry, this was plain and simple jealousy.

"Cleaning, all done?"

"Yeah, that's right."

After confirming that Kenneth was putting away the cleaning supplies, Latina went into the kitchen, climbed up onto a stool, and washed off her dishcloth. Since she couldn't wring it out very well with her scrawny arms, she ended up leaving it at the sink.

She then dragged along the stool, which was meant for her personal use, back to its "home base" and sat down on top of it. She held a small knife—also made for her at some point—in her tiny hands and awkwardly started peeling vegetables. Considering her pace, she was "taking up time" more than "helping," but Kenneth wasn't hard-hearted, so he sat down next to her and began silently peeling as well.

Though she was still clumsy, it was certainly impressive that she could do it herself after having just been taught how. But according to Kenneth, he didn't break his firm stance and simply watched over her. This was quite a difference compared to Dale; it took everything he had just to resist the urge to get involved without even thinking about it.

"If it bugs you that much, then you'd be better off just not watching."

"Then I'd miss out on getting to see Latina grow up," Dale declared bluntly.

Rita, who was sorting through documents, wore a half-hearted expression on her face.

Having finished peeling, Latina apparently decided it was time for a break. She grabbed the picture books she had left in the corner of the pantry and took them to a table in the shop.

She had two books with her: the first was the one originally used to teach her words, while the second one was a significantly harder storybook.

"Dale, book, read."

"Right."

Because Dale had picked out the book for him to read aloud to Latina, he'd figured it would be too hard for her to read alone. But in this short time, even if it was only stutteringly, she had become able to read through it by herself. Normally she read silently, but when Dale was there she read it aloud, apparently intending for him to correct her. She also seemed happy to show the fruits of her labor as well.

Once she finished reading through to the end, Latina received Dale's approval, then opened up the other picture book alongside a notebook. In rough, childish letters, she was diligently practicing her writing.

"She started studying this on her own, without anyone telling her to, right?"

"Yeah. When Latina asked for paper, I figured she wanted to draw a picture or something. I never imagined it was for writing practice."

"There aren't any kids around Latina's age at the school they hold at the temple of Akhdar, are there?"

"Right. But she knew how to hold a pen to begin with. Kenneth had to teach her how to use a knife at first, but she was able to use a pen without asking anyone how. Maybe she was raised in a pretty good environment."

Even though Latina was now able to talk, she still didn't say much about herself. She only answered with the absolute minimum required. Sure enough, the corpse in the forest belonged to her father. After her horn was broken, they had left their old home together. And that place, where she had been born, was a devil village. That was all she would say.

Considering how sharp she was, it wouldn't be odd for her to know all other sorts of things. In all likelihood, she was also aware of what her having a broken horn meant. She may have been worried that if she talked about herself in detail, she'd be driven out, like she had been from her old village. If she was willing to talk, Dale definitely wanted to know, but he had no intention of dragging it out of her.

Even though they'd only spent a short time together, he couldn't possibly think of her as the wicked sort of person worthy of being called a criminal, which meant that the "crime" was something that had nothing to do with her character. He couldn't say if it was political, or perhaps religious in nature, but either way, it was most definitely irrational. And that was most likely why her father chose to leave the village alongside her.

"Dale, what's wrong?"

While he was thinking, he had apparently been making a gloomy face. At some point, Latina had tilted her head in confusion and looked up at him.

"Hmm? It's nothing. You've gotten good at speaking, Latina," Dale said while patting her head, causing her to break out in a happy smile.

"Latina is glad she can talk. She worked hard."

"Is that so?"

Seeing her innocent smile, Dale's expression softened as well. Dale realized that he'd become able to break out in an earnest smile as well since he started living with Latina. He'd smirked upon hearing stupid stories from Rita and Kenneth in the past, but he'd never broken out in such a calm and gentle smile before. This was a clear change brought about by Latina's arrival.

In the intervals between lunch, her nap, and her snack, Latina enjoyed her free time. On the days that Dale wasn't out, she played near him. Every now and again, she'd gaze out the entrance to the shop, but at least thus far, she hadn't wandered out on her own. She'd gone out on walks about the neighborhood with Rita, Dale, or Kenneth before, but she still didn't understand the lay of the land.

But when the time came for Kenneth to start his evening prep-work, Latina would head to the kitchen and follow him around once more. Every time Dale went to look in on this, he'd see her super-diligent face which seemed to say, "I'm giving it my all!" and end up walking away in low spirits, unable to say anything.

With that same serious look on her face, Latina was currently tackling the task of mashing a large pile of potatoes.

"Calm down a little," Rita, who was carrying a mug of ale, told Dale.

At the Dancing Ocelot, customers paid up their accounts when they got what they ordered. This was to prevent people from shirking payment. However, that rule didn't apply to the regulars, who were allowed to settle their accounts at the end. In Dale's case, if he didn't square up, then it was added to his rent. The sound of coins jingling in Rita's apron told of her skill at handling both orders and billing. In the morning, incidentally, in order to more efficiently handle the busy period, there was a simple entry fee instead.

Dale took offense to Rita's words but was unable to come up with a decent comeback.

While this was going on, Latina came out of the kitchen carrying a tray, and thanks to the weight, she was a bit unsteady. In an instant, the hustle and bustle of the shop quieted down.

Over the course of the past week, the regulars had all become aware of Latina's presence. Though she was tiny, she never fooled around while darting about the shop, so they all noticed her even if they weren't trying to. On top of it, there was something incredibly charming about the young girl.

Latina slowly and carefully walked forward, step by step. This was her greatest trial as of late: bringing Dale his dinner. She wanted to do it, but that required her carrying it all the way to the customer. Thanks to her pride and repeated practice, however, she was able to do it.

When she'd safely made it to Dale with the tray, she broke out in a wide grin. It was a smile that truly said, "Mission complete!"

A silent applause seemed to come from her audience. When she'd tripped partway there two days ago, she'd looked so shocked that you would have thought the world had ended. She became so depressed that it would have been preferable for her to have just cried. The people watching her naturally felt the pressure as well.

"Dale, dinner, here!"

Dale took the tray and brought it up onto of the table. After seeing that through, Latina returned to the kitchen and brought out her own meal. Thanks to the clear difference in size, this time her footsteps were obviously lighter.

Having sat down beside Dale, she proudly said, "Latina, today, made potatoes. Eat, Dale."

"Right. You did great today too, Latina."

Latina pointing to the mountain of mashed potatoes and reporting what she did with a smile, while Dale in turn praised her, had become the routine for the last few days. It had also lately become a trend in the Dancing Ocelot that after these two had such an exchange, sales of whatever Latina had helped with increased.

As Kenneth checked during the brief breaks he had between cooking countless orders, he saw Latina happily enjoying her meal again today, which made him grin broadly.

Latina gave it her all each and every day. She wanted to make a meal for Dale at some point, which made for a powerful motivator. And so, she was working on this seriously. Kenneth was fond of people who worked hard.

The young girl was certainly putting more than enough effort into the task, and thanks to that, she was seeing results. To Kenneth, she was an "apprentice" worth teaching.

The reason Latina was able to spend time in this shop with such a calm expression on her face was because it was the "safe place that Dale brought her to." Dale was the only one who didn't know that. She was able to be so unconditionally relaxed precisely because he was by her side. Dale hadn't seen that when he wasn't around, she frantically looked about, and even felt threatened at times.

"It's not so bad for both of them, having someone to rely on. Even for Dale," muttered Dale's self-proclaimed "big bro," a man who realized he'd come to earn a level of trust worthy of that title, as he served up the contents of a pot.

The girl was in a pinch.

"What should Latina do?"

She worriedly glanced about at the people coming and going. Right now, she wasn't in the southern district of Kreuz, where she lived. She had accompanied Kenneth when he went out to replenish stock, and had come to the eastern district.

This was only her second time visiting this part of town. The first time, she still hadn't understood the language at all, so even though she had been interested in her surroundings, she hadn't left Dale's side at all. As a result, things had gone fine then. This time, though, she was completely enraptured by the things around her.

As it was an important waypoint, Kreuz was abundant with all sorts of goods; it was absolutely overflowing with all sorts of items that Latina hadn't seen before and didn't even know how they were used. The various shops, lined up in rows, all had their own ways to grab the attention of passersby.

This part of town, which had an entirely different feel compared to the southern district, captured Latina's attention. To start with, the girl had curiosity in spades, and she couldn't help that that curiosity won out over her wariness and concentration. Thanks to that, she had lost sight of Kenneth before she'd even realized it.

Latina promised to stay with Kenneth… Will Dale be angry? she thought, becoming more and more depressed. Clearly at a loss, she didn't know at all what to do. *Latina may never see him again. What should she do?*

She didn't want to be left alone again. Even though she was surrounded by so many people, she couldn't help but feel tormented by an overwhelming feeling of isolation. She couldn't stop herself from thinking that these were bad people.

Latina hates this... What should she do? If she doesn't make it back... if she doesn't get back... Her mind was spinning in circles with such thoughts.

Though she was smart, Latina was still young, so her being driven by emotion rather than logic was a natural reaction. But right now, there was no one to tell her that.

Perhaps because of her experience in the forest, where she had to take care of herself rather than waiting for someone to save her, she didn't realize that the best thing to do when you're lost is to wait in one spot.

Latina took a guess at the direction she should go and started running. If she had stayed put just a little longer, she would've seen Kenneth return in a panic.

Latina ended up turning several corners and entering a block she'd genuinely never seen before.

"...Where is this?"

There was no way that she could've known, but this area was known for having a particularly high concentration of artisans, even for the eastern district. Lined up one after another were houses that served both as residences and workshops. Compared to the eastern district's main street, it was an area with a more working-class sort of feel to it, with many complicated, crisscrossing alleyways; to people other than residents, it may well have felt like a labyrinth. That was certainly the case for Latina, who didn't even understand how she got here, even when she looked back over her shoulder.

"…What should Latina do?" she muttered to herself, utterly at a loss.

"Who are you?"

Hearing a voice from behind, Latina jumped in surprise. When she turned around, she saw a group of boys standing around. They frowned at the sight of this girl they didn't recognize.

"Where are you from? I've never seen you before," said the biggest boy in the group while steadily approaching Latina.

"…"

Not knowing how to reply, she retreated a bit in order to distance herself. Seeing that, the expression on his face only grew more and more distrusting. The large boy named Rudy, the quiet boy next to him with a round face, and the boy behind him with light-brown hair spoke in turn.

"I've never seen hair that color before. Are you the kid of some sort of noble?"

"That's not it, Rudy. If she were, she'd be wearing a gown."

"That's right. But still, her hair's an unusual color. It doesn't quite look like gold or silver."

"If a girl like her moved in, then there's no way we wouldn't have heard rumors about it."

"Then you're an outsider?!"

When Latina heard the gruff tone of Rudy's voice, she recoiled again.

Why is he mad? Is… Latina strange, somehow?

What should Latina do…? Latina doesn't know why he's mad.

"That's not cool, Rudy. You made her cry."

"She's the one who won't talk, even though we're asking her questions!"

Though the round-faced boy tried to stop him, Rudy kept stomping towards Latina. Now completely in a panic, her face turning pale, Latina tried to flee.

"Why are you running?! You're acting fishy!"

However, due to the difference in their physiques, Rudy soon overtook and captured her.

"…! **! ****!"

Hearing the yell that Latina let out the second Rudy grabbed her arm left the boys stupefied.

"What did she say?"

"Maybe she's a foreigner…"

As the boys glanced at each other, they had already lost all their anger, leaving behind only confusion. But because Latina was still panicking, she didn't realize that.

Desperately twisting about, she screamed, "**, **! ****!"

"What are you doing?!"

A girl about the same age as the boys came flying out of a nearby house at the sound of Latina's screaming. As soon as she saw Latina's ghostly pale face, she leaped right at the boys.

"You're the absolute worst, picking on such a little girl!"

"Gah! Cut it out, Chloe!"

"You got it all wrong!"

The brown-haired boy swiftly distanced himself, but the other two fell victim to Chloe's punches. Latina stopped panicking and absentmindedly stared in admiration at the girl. Her intervention had rescued Latina.

"Does it hurt? Are you alright?" asked Latina.

"They're fine! Just slap some spit on there and it'll heal up fine!"

"No one asked you, Chloe!"

With a worried look on her face, Latina squatted down and stared at the two boys Chloe had beaten and kicked, Rudy and Marcel the round-faced boy.

"This is because Latina didn't respond… She's sorry…"

"It's our fault for scaring you…" Marcel said with a strained laugh, but Latina only looked even more apologetic.

The look on her face grew serious, and she thrust her tiny hand out towards him. She moistened her lips and carefully began a chant.

"Oh light of heaven, grant this request by my name, and please heal those who have been wounded. 《Healing Light》"

A gentle light flowed out from Latina's hand, causing the other children's eyes to go wide.

Latina then used the same recovery magic on Rudy as well, and then, with a frown on her face, she suddenly sat down.

"Are you alright?"

"Latina's alright. Just a little tired," she answered Chloe with a smile. Taking that as their chance, the boys excitedly crowded around Latina.

"That's amazing! You can use magic?!"

"It really is incredible, to be able to use magic when you're so young! Who taught you?"

"That's the first time I've ever seen anyone use it!"

Seeing Latina shake in response to their vigorous excitement, Chloe took a step forward and shot them a glare. The boys stopped instantly, and Latina peeked out from behind Chloe's back.

"Amazing? But Latina can only use one simple healing spell," she said as she tilted her head in complete confusion. "Is using magic amazing?"

"Hardly anyone around town can use it. It's pretty much just the people who work at temples or for the feudal lord, or at one of the big companies. Outside of that, it's just adventurers, I guess," explained the brown-haired boy, Anthony, and Latina nodded her head to show that she understood.

Dale's an adventurer. So he can use magic.

And then suddenly, she remembered that she was lost.

"Latina is lost… She doesn't know the way back…"

"Where did you come from, Latina?"

"The Ocelot shop… in the south…" responded the disheartened girl. The children glanced at one another.

"Ocelot?"

"There aren't that many shops in the south."

"Could it be that one? The one with the green flags."

"That shop for adventurers?"

Hearing those words, Latina's expression brightened up. "Yeah. Lots of adventurers come to the shop."

With that response, the children looked at each other again. A shop for adventurers was a dangerous place where people who took on hazardous work gathered. Their parents had forbidden them from playing in that part of the southern district.

But this was to help someone out. This definitely wasn't just because they wanted to go see.

Ultimately, forbidding children from doing something only makes them more interested.

†

This occurred in the southern district a little before Latina opened up to the children in the eastern district:

"Latina's lost?!" A shriek so loud it even reached outside the shop emanated from the Dancing Ocelot.

When Kenneth realized Latina wasn't there, he had hurriedly looked everywhere for her. But by then, she was already nowhere to be found. However, he couldn't keep looking for her forever; he also needed to carry the supplies back to the shop.

After asking a number of his acquaintances in the eastern district for their help, he hurriedly returned to the Dancing Ocelot. After all, that was where her father was, and he was the one who most needed to know the situation.

"Yeah, I'm really sorry. I took my eyes of her for a second when I was negotiating, and…"

Kenneth and Dale had both let their guard down. Latina was an incredibly clever girl, and the two couldn't deny they had unconsciously come to think that she could handle this much. She was well-behaved, so surely she wouldn't wander off. That was just an excuse the adults came up with on their own.

Naturally, adults and children had differing points of view. To start with, the way they saw the world was not the same. Adult thinking could not grasp how children behaved.

"Ah, no, it's… She's already lost, so no matter what we do now, what's done is done. It's… Aaaaaagh! If this was going to happen, then I should've learned some search magic! Apologize to Latina, past-me, for saying that stuff was unnecessary! I'm sorry, I'm sorry, I'm sorry… No, that's right. Right now, Latina's… What should I do? What should I do? Oh, i-if I send out a request, then I can have the adventurers in town look for her!" Dale went on and on and on.

"How about going to look for her, to start with?" said Rita.

"That's it!"

While he may have been acting irrationally, seeing Dale so amusingly agitated actually helped those around him cool down. When Dale's panic reached its peak, Rita told him what to do, and he immediately flew out of the shop.

"Um… Rita?" Kenneth asked.

"In addition to Dale, I also sent word of what Latina looks like out about town. And plenty of the gatekeepers are regulars here, so even if someone's dumb enough to try and kidnap her, they'll be stopped at the walls. I get the feeling that even if she is lost, that girl could manage to do something about it on her own, but…"

Looking at his wife after she sent Dale off, Kenneth thought that she seemed exceptionally calm. A big reason why Rita was able to remain so composed was because Latina had gotten lost in an exceptionally safe area, even for the eastern district.

She then faced the various adventurers engrossed in idle talk about the shop.

"Anyone who helps out with the search drinks for free tonight. And if you find her, then I'll give you a reward. Even if you don't find her, be sure to come back here by the hour of Saj—before sunset. How does that sound?"

"Well, I guess it'll kill some time."

"It wouldn't be so bad having Dale owe me one, either."

Saying such things in response, the regulars got up out of their seats. Latina was becoming a special person to the regulars as well.

When Latina at last returned, surrounded by the children from the eastern district, the sun had not yet set.

"Rita!" Latina passed through the door with a smile and ran towards her, only to stop suddenly. "Rita, Latina's sorry she got lost… Where's Kenneth?"

"He's worrying about you. Go show him that you're back," Rita replied, pointing towards the kitchen. To be honest, the sight of her husband being so worried about Latina that he couldn't properly concentrate on his work had left her at a loss.

When he saw Latina hurrying towards the kitchen, Kenneth dropped the pot he was holding. A loud crashing sound filled the air.

"Kenneth, Latina's sorry. She got lost, so she couldn't keep her promise…"

Seeing her so depressed as she earnestly apologized, and knowing that he was at fault, Kenneth couldn't bring himself to scold her. He simply felt relieved and patted her tiny head.

"I'm glad you're alright."

Kenneth scooped up the dejected Latina in his arms and headed into the shop, where a group of children looked up at him. As kids didn't usually come into the store, Kenneth was frankly a little surprised. "Who are they?"

"These kids brought Latina back here," said Rita, having talked to the one girl in the group.

"Then we've gotta give them a reward…"

"Friends help each other out, that's how it is!" the girl objected in response. Latina tilted her small head in confusion.

"I see, so Latina's made some friends. It's already a little late today, but you'll have to play plenty with her next time," said Rita, with a wide and gentle smile on her face, the sort that she didn't usually make. She then opened up the jar of cookies that Kenneth had prepared for Latina's snacks, and skillfully put together a bundle for each child.

"We really are grateful that you brought Latina back." On bended knee, so as to meet the children at eye level, she offered these words of thanks alongside the cookies. Having an adult like Rita act

81

so polite towards them, the children exchanged nervous and fidgety glances, but it seemed they didn't entirely dislike the treatment.

When Chloe and company headed back home, Latina stood in the door to the shop, seeing them off by waving her hand.

As the hour of Saj approached, the regulars returned to the Dancing Ocelot, and Latina bowed her head to each and every one of them.

"Sorry for worrying you…"

"As long as you're alright, then it's no problem, little lady."

"…Thank you for looking for Latina." Latina gave another bow of her head to the regular, who laughed and waved it off.

When he first returned to the shop, Latina had greeted him with a smile, but now that he saw her from behind, it was obvious that she was disheartened. Watching her pace back and forth to the entrance of the shop, he became depressed as well.

Seeing Latina acting differently than she usually did made not only the regulars who knew what was going on but also the customers who didn't know anything just keep drinking in silence. That was the sort of mood in the shop when Dale at last returned.

When he opened the door, he was out of breath and dripping in sweat. "Rita! What's happened since I…?" While asking if there was any new information, he suddenly realized that the person in question was staring up at him. "Latina!"

Her response to Dale calling out her name in joy was a flow of tears.

"…?!"

As Dale panicked and fell to his knees, speechless, Latina shed even more teardrops. "L-Latina?!"

"L-Latina's sorry… She's sorry… She's so sorry that she didn't keep her promise…" said Latina, sobbing convulsively as she apologized. "Dale, are you mad because Latina was bad?"

"I'm not mad! Not at all! I was just worried!" Dale shook his head vigorously, but Latina only kept on talking, shaking her head in denial as well.

"It's okay if you're mad. Latina was bad, after all… B-But, Latina was scared. She was scared she wouldn't make it back."

The tears were now steadily overflowing from her big grey eyes. With the last bit of composure he had left, Dale realized that this was the first time he'd seen the young girl cry.

"Latina doesn't wanna be alone again, Dale… It's fine if you're mad at Latina, but she wants to stay with you…"

Apparently, Latina had thought on this a lot after she'd made it back to the Dancing Ocelot. During that time, she must have remembered the helplessness and anxiety she'd felt when she was lost, leaving her awash in strong emotions. She felt she absolutely needed to apologize, but once she had, she was swept away by that feeling of unease… Or at least, that was what Dale guessed later on, after he calmed down.

For now, as he was a complete and utter wreck, all he could do was hug the sobbing Latina tight. At this point, the fact that she was already sobbing became her reason for crying more.

For a time, she couldn't talk and just kept on weeping. As Latina continued to cry, Dale was only able to keep himself together because he knew that this would eventually end when she tired herself out. Dale held Latina in his arms as she became exhausted and nodded off, and the nearby customers shot him strained smiles.

This was the moment that a new drinking tale for the shop, which would later come to be called the "panic and wailing incident," was born.

†

After that day, Latina began playing with the children from the eastern district.

The shop in the southern district faced out on the street, and it had a more wholesome feel to it than the other stores that served adventurers. But even so, it was no place for children to be playing. And yet, Dale started to see children in the area as of late, which he found odd. But when he heard the story from Kenneth, Rita, and Latina, he figured out what was happening.

The children from the eastern district had been coming to pick up Latina, who was unfamiliar with the town, playing with her, and then escorting her back when they were done. Apparently, the kids also knew that this part of the southern district wasn't entirely safe, so they always came as a group.

It's not as though Dale thought it'd be alright to keep Latina in the shop forever, and he had also been worried that she was only interacting with adults like himself. And in that way, these children from the eastern district were a godsend.

As a result, he casually remarked, "I'm glad you made some friends, Latina."

Her response of, "What does 'friends' mean, Dale?" though, was something he hadn't expected in the least.

"Huh? Um… did you not have any friends before, Latina?"

"…? Latina doesn't really understand what 'friends' means. Chloe also said Latina was her friend, but Latina doesn't get it."

As Latina tilted her head in confusion, Dale let out a, "Hmm…"

Since Latina was carefree and he didn't sense any sort of uneasy gloom from her, Dale figured that she wasn't necessarily treated horribly back in her home village. And yet, she had a broken horn. And so she had become possibly the greatest possible sort of target for contempt amongst devils.

He had no clue if he was stepping on a landmine here or not.

"Um… Latina, did you not ever play with kids around your age before?"

"Playing together? Do you mean with family?"

"No, not family. Didn't you ever play with kids from other houses?"

Latina tilted her head in confusion again.

"Latina… only ever had family and adults around."

With that, Dale remembered that devils were a race with a long lifespan and a low birthrate. There wouldn't be many kids around in the first place.

"Hmm… Friends refers to people other than your family who you can play and talk with. They're usually around the same age as you." He added the last part so she wouldn't think of him, Rita, and Kenneth as her "friends." "And out of those sorts of people, they're the ones who come to like you."

He couldn't really say that was the way the world worked, but he wanted to raise this honest child while letting her think that. That's what Dale thought.

"Chloe likes Latina?"

"I doubt anybody would want to become friends with someone they weren't fond of."

After thinking on Dale's words for a while, Latina's expression lit up.

"Latina likes Chloe, too. She's glad Chloe called Latina her friend."

"I see."

Seeing the happy look on her face made Dale worry a little as he patted Latina's head. He thought he should ask the meaning of what she said before, so he chose his words carefully and spoke.

"…What sort of people were you around before?"

"Latina doesn't know. How should she put it?"

Having had this question, which he'd needed to steel himself to ask, answered with another question, Dale at last realized his mistake. Latina had fundamentally no words to use for explaining things.

"Um, about your family… Did you have any siblings?"

"Siblings?"

"Kids in your family who have the same parents. A boy would be your brother, while a girl would be your sister, and they can be older or younger than you. That's what 'siblings' means."

"Latina had an older brother and sister. But no younger ones," Latina responded, having heard Dale's explanation.

"What sort of people were the adults?"

"Don't know. Latina didn't meet other people much, and she didn't talk to them. She was usually with her family," answered Latina, getting a little depressed in the process. This seemed about the right place to stop. After all, these didn't seem to be happy memories for her.

Having decided that, Dale was about to put an end to the discussion.

"That's why Latina's so happy now, because she gets to spend lots of time with Dale." The words that she said, while seeming to somewhat embarrass her, landed a critical hit. The smile she gave

Dale now wouldn't lose out to even the one she made when eating her beloved sweets. "Latina likes Chloe, but she loves Dale lots and lots more."

"I love you too, Latina! You really are cute!" Latina's face truly looked happy as he said those words and suddenly hugged her.

If this were a plot to make me drop the matter, then that'd be an ominous premonition... But if it were an ugly, wicked woman who was trying to deceive me, it would be no problem!

Regardless of these ridiculous thoughts, Dale seemed to be truly blissful at this moment.

"Latina's so cute that I just don't want to go to work!"

"Are you still saying that, you moron?"

As Dale uttered his typical line with a terribly serious look on his face, Rita gave her normal, casual response back.

"I don't waaaaaaanna! I won't make it back tonight, and I don't even know how many days I'll be gone! How am I *supposed* to handle leaving Latina so I can go deal with those demonic old geezers?!"

He was slumped across the counter, and the sound of his fists pounding on it grew louder and louder. Needless to say, when he started stomping his feet as well, he looked just like a spoiled brat throwing a fit. That just went to show how stressful he found the situation.

"If it bugs you that much, then why don't you take Latina with you to the capital?"

"Well y'see, if I let those bastards in the capital take care of Latina, who knows what could happen... I can't imagine anything but trouble coming from that."

Dale snapped back to his senses in an instant, then fell limp across the counter again.

"I get it... It's for work, so I've gotta do it. And knowing that Latina's waiting for me, that'll motivate me more than ever. Plus, Latina seems to have made some friends, so that should help keep her distracted while she's holding down the fort... So I get it, already!"

He clenched his fists tightly and his knuckles turned white, as if to show how deep the emotions driving the action were.

"But still, I just don't *wanna*!"

Ah, he really was pathetic.

In response to Dale's outpouring, Rita looked at him as if to say he was a hopeless case.

"If you get that there's nothing you can do about it, then how about bringing Latina back a souvenir that you think she'll like from the capital?"

As Dale turned to face Rita, he looked as if a light had gone off in his head.

"You have to worry about sizes when it comes to clothes, and it wouldn't be long before she'd outgrow them, so don't go with that. Oh right, she's really fond of sweets, so how about taking a look at some famous shops in the capital?"

"Souvenirs… Souvenirs, huh…?"

Dale went to the capital for work so often that he hadn't even considered the idea of buying souvenirs. The closest he got was when Kenneth occasionally asked him to pick up things that were hard to get in Kreuz while he was there.

Latina would be all smiles when she saw the latest popular sweets from the capital, and she'd definitely say, "Thank you!" in that cute voice of hers. Definitely. There was no doubt. She may even throw in an "I love you, Dale!" What should he do? She was just too cute! He may even be able to survive on that cuteness alone.

"I think I may be able to give it my all."

"Yeah, right. Good for you," said Rita, who had already returned to work and was no longer looking at him.

On the morning of the day that Dale was heading to the capital, Latina got up early to see him off. The morning sun hadn't completely risen yet, and it was long before she would normally wake up.

"Don't push yourself. How about just going back to sleep?" Dale told her, but she shook her head and crawled out of bed.

And yet, she was still pretty sleepy. It would be rather dangerous to let her try to go down the stairs like this, even more so considering their room was in the attic and reached via ladder.

Dale lifted her up with a strained smile.

Even though not too much time had passed since they first met, he could tell that she'd managed to regain a relieving amount of weight.

Latina was currently still half-asleep and kept nodding off, then forcing herself back awake.

"I'm sorry, Latina... You're going to be holding down the fort for a bit. Do you think you can handle it?"

Feeling Dale's palm on her back, her eyes shot open, and she responded with a serious look of determination on her face. "Latina will give it her all. She'll be here with Rita and Kenneth. So please, come back."

"Right, and I'll bring a souvenir back with me. So take care, and watch the place for me."

He gave her one last, firm hug and set her down. When they reached the entrance to the shop, Kenneth took charge of Latina.

"Take care of Latina, alright?"

"Yeah. And you be sure not to push yourself too hard."

He'd never seen Dale respond with a smile like that before.

"Right, I'm off."

"Dale, take care. Be careful on your work!"

While thoroughly savoring those words from Latina, Dale set off from the town of Kreuz.

…Right, I'll give it my all.

†

The trip from Kreuz to Ausblick, the capital of the nation of Laband, was three days by horse or one week by carriage. The road was well-maintained, as it was an important route for the country and a great number of merchants and travelers came and went along it.

However, Dale was heading in the direction of the woods on the outskirts of town, rather than towards this grand highway.

In an open meadow outside of Kreuz, there was a large beast resting its wings—a flying dragon. Flying dragons were considered small for a subspecies of dragons, which were classified as magical beasts. In addition, they possessed the ability to fly, which other dragons did not have.

Even for a flying dragon, the specimen in this field was rather tiny, and from the scarlet equipment attached to its body, it was obvious even from a distance that it was in the service of the country of Laband.

By its side was a young man pacing back and forth, unable to calm his nerves. The man's clothes were the same scarlet color the dragon was wearing. That uniform and his simple, jet-black armor identified him as a dragon knight, with the ability to control a flying dragon using the rare magical attribute of "Center."

"Ugh, what should I do, Titi? He's supposed to be really hard to deal with…" the man grumbled to his partner next to him.

The gentle-natured female dragon responded with a cry of "*Coo?*"

As the pair wasn't cut out for combat, their main duty was transporting goods and people, and because flying dragons weren't suited for traveling in the dark, they had spent the night waiting here for their passenger, who wanted to go to the capital.

"Apparently, he's an adventurer who has a contract with the duke. I hear the knight I replaced offended him and got demoted to a frontier post… We finally got a high-paying job in the capital, but… Ugh, are we gonna be alright…?"

His current mission was to escort *that* adventurer to the capital.

Despite the adventurer's young age, he'd already racked up some impressive achievements and possessed a great deal of influence, as he held the favor of the duke who served as the prime minister, the right-hand man of the King of Laband. Even though he was ultimately just an adventurer favored by the duke, if the knight upset him, the duke would hear about it right away. Normally, the nation's leading authorities would pay no heed to the words of a mere adventurer, but apparently *this* adventurer was an exception.

Rumor had it that the previous dragon knight had made light of this adventurer because of how young he was, and that had earned the knight the wrath of his superiors. He'd been sent off to the frontier by order of the duke himself.

The duke had dispatched a flying dragon just for this man who lived in Kreuz, so it was abundantly clear how much he was favored.

"…! Titi, he's here!"

Worrying for her master, the dragon gave a "*Coo*" to show that she understood.

A young man in a long black leather coat approached as the morning sun shone behind him. The dull, metallic sparkle coming from his left arm must have been his gauntlet-shaped magical device. He also wore a longsword at his waist, making him a perfect fit for the description that the dragon knight had been given.

This young adventurer was skilled enough that he could cut down even the knight's partner, Titi, with a single swing of his sword. Even if Titi naturally wasn't overly aggressive, she was still a dragon, so normal adventurers would have needed to come at her as a team.

"Under order of His Excellency, Duke Eldstedt, I have come here to meet you!"

"Right. I'm Dale Reki," responded the young man to the knight's low, quiet voice, perfectly relaxed as he looked over him and his partner. Feeling an aura he couldn't hope to match coming off the adventurer, who looked even younger than he was, the dragon knight gulped.

"Please, come this way."

After guiding him to the saddle on Titi's back, the knight took the luggage the man had brought and tied it down securely. Though the saddle on a flying dragon was far, far higher up than it would be on a horse, the young man easily pulled himself up without losing his balance. As he fastened his belt to finish preparing for flight, it was clear that he was used to the process.

The dragon knight hurried to his own saddle and grasped the reins. These reins were made from a special material that could easily transmit his mana. By grasping them, the knight could give detailed instructions to his dragon, and they also conveyed the dragon's thoughts back to him. It was a dragon knight's most important and precious piece of equipment.

"Let's go, Titi," he said, delivering the short command with his mana. Following his instruction, the dragon spread out her wings, let out a peculiar cry of "*Coo-loo-loo*," and gathered up the wind mana from the area. Using both the wind mana that enveloped her and the traits she possessed as a natural-born flier, the dragon lifted her giant frame off the ground with a single flap of her wings. With a second flap, she soared high into the heavens, and with a third, she began moving towards the capital.

At a flying dragon's speed, the journey to the capital wouldn't take more than half a day. That was one of the reasons those capable of serving as dragon knights were paid a high salary. Methods for flying through the air were extremely limited. It was impossible to accomplish with magic alone, and so it was a special privilege limited to those who were born to fly through the heavens.

As a result, it was considered a talent of particular military significance and was strictly regulated. When it came to flying dragons, the nation held a great deal of authority over things like breeding laws and the maintenance of specialized tools, such as their reins. There were no such things as privatized flying dragon rides. In order to fly a dragon, you had no choice but to act in service of the country.

Ugh, this is awkward...

Titi called out "*Coo?*" apparently worried about her rider, who wasn't acting like himself. It was entirely calm on the back of the flying dragon, despite the whirl of wind mana whipping through the surrounding sky. It was like being in the eye of a hurricane.

And yet, the knight deplored that now. If there were at least a gentle breeze, then that would feel good on his sweat-drenched brow.

Are we really going to go the whole way without talking? This is so awkward...

The knight had no confidence that he'd be able to withstand nearly half a day of this silent pressure. Feeling the presence of the man behind him, his throat went bone-dry.

He reached underneath his own saddle and took something out. As he'd grown accustomed to doing so, he was able to skillfully remove the contents with a single hand and pop one into his mouth. There was no deep meaning to his actions when he kept on going and offered the container to the man behind him. In fact, in his current state, the dragon knight was unable to consider the deep meaning of anything at all.

"Would you care to try some, sir?"

"...Candy?"

Completely petrified, he cried out in a quiet voice, *I'm done foooooooor!!*

The greatest taboo when it came to Dale Reki was treating him like a child.

The dragon knight forced a nervous smile, not realizing that the man behind him couldn't see his face, and kept on talking, hoping to turn the situation around.

"These are the talk of the capital nowadays! They all have different flavors based on what color they are. And they come in all sorts of truly vibrant colors! They're like beautiful jewels, making them popular with everyone from commoners to nobles!"

With that, the bottle was snatched from his hands.

It seemed he had managed to grab the adventurer's interest, at least for the time being. Glimpsing a possible way out, the dragon knight decided to press further.

"The bottle is a work of art too, isn't it? The detailed design extends even to the lid. And apparently, it's become popular with women and children to use the empty bottle to hold small items! Furthermore, since it comes in small, medium, and large sizes, it makes for a great gift that can be tailored to suit your budget and needs. They're perfect for any type of consumer!" As the dragon knight desperately spouted off lines that made him sound like a candy salesman, he wondered what he would see if he turned around.

Thinking about it, I've actually never bought candy for Latina before. If she put one in her mouth, her little cheeks would puff out, right? And the colors are pretty, which seems like the sort of thing that'd make a girl happy. When I bought Latina hair accessories, she was fixated on the sparkly ones. Even if she's tiny, she's still a girl, so I'm sure she'd like them. Oh right, one of Latina's friends is a girl, too. I'll need to get some for her as well. Latina would probably be happy if she and her friend got the same thing. And then…

At the very least, the dragon knight would've realized he was far more on-edge than he needed to be in regards to Dale during this trip to the capital.

There's no doubt that if Dale was still his old self, what the dragon knight had done would've been like stepping right on a landmine. But to Dale now, the offense was slight enough that it wasn't even worth thinking about. The adventurer just didn't have enough space in his mind for such things nowadays.

Though no one would ever know it, Latina had helped save the future of a single young man with great promise.

†

When they at last arrived at Laband's capital, Ausblick, the flying dragon began its descent. After the dragon knight communicated with a soldier on the ground using the light from magical devices, they landed on a dedicated platform. As you could be shot down if you approached the capital carelessly, it was necessary to follow the proper procedures.

Once he set foot on the ground, Dale approached the carriage that was waiting for him as always, not even bothering to so much as glance back at the dragon or the knight. The driver opened the carriage door for him without needing to ask who he was.

Though it wasn't overly flashy, there wasn't anyone in the capital who wouldn't recognize the family crest that was affixed to this luxurious coach.

The Ducal House Eldstedt were descendants of the king who founded the nation, and they had married into the royal family many times in the past, making them a line of foremost pedigree in Laband. They weren't overly haughty, despite being famous for producing talented heirs one after another, with the present duke serving as the current prime minister.

It would be no exaggeration to say that they were the second-greatest authority in the nation. It was precisely because the king and the duke were able to focus on governing together rather than pandering to one another that the country was so unwaveringly powerful.

In a district where noble mansions stood in a row, one castle had a clearly different feel to it and stood out from the rest of the luxurious buildings. While it was beautiful and possessed vast grounds, it was also built to be solid and practical. This was the castle of the Eldstedt family.

The carriage Dale was taking rolled onto the grounds of that residence and glided to a gentle stop in front of the entrance. As if they knew the precise time he would arrive, the servants who had been awaiting him opened the doors and greeted him.

As he descended from the carriage, Dale's expression didn't change in the least. That calm and collected look told of his skill as a first-rate adventurer and left a deep impression on those who saw it.

In one room of the residence:

"Long time no see, Gregor. So, you gonna introduce me to your fiancée?"

"Hmph, very well, Dale. So you wish me to cut you down, then?"

With that reprehensible exchange, the elegant atmosphere evaporated.

Right now, they were in Gregor's personal chamber. As if reflecting its owner's personality, the high quality of the first-class furnishings was almost palpable, but the interior design was utterly lacking in splendor.

Gregor was the third son of the duke and was his youngest child. However, unlike his siblings, he was the son of the duke's second wife, and because she was a foreigner from a remote Eastern nation, his backing within the country was rather weak. The first son, who was noticeably older than him, had already married and had a child. Considering the circumstances, Gregor's chances of becoming his father's successor had quickly evaporated.

Thanks to the strong influence of his mother's blood, Gregor was a fearless-looking young man with straight black hair (currently tied up in a ponytail), and he had a strong foreign feel to his appearance. He was half a head taller than Dale, and today his slender body was dressed in high-class clothing befitting a noble, which was unusual for him.

While Gregor diligently studied his own nation, he also polished his foreign sword techniques, and he had his eye on possibly using his sword skills to become an adventurer in the near future. As he wasn't particularly attached to his position as a noble, he felt no need to force himself to become part of some other household.

It was thanks to those circumstances that he had become close to a mere adventurer like Dale. It also helped that they were the same age and recognized one another's strengths, even if their specialties were different.

"Rose isn't even my fiancée to begin with."

"So about souvenirs… I want to find something that'd make a little girl happy. You don't know any young women besides that fiancée of yours, right?"

"Alright, stand up. I'll cut you down with a stroke of my blade."

The "fiancée" Dale was teasing him about was not someone he was actually engaged to. Gregor and Rose had loved one another since they were both young, but there were a great number of issues that stood in the way of them becoming officially engaged.

While she was renowned as a beauty without peer, she hadn't yet been used as a pawn in a political marriage and rarely appeared in high society. Instead, she silently spent her time in the depths of the estate.

She was most definitely one of the reasons that Gregor couldn't simply discard his position as a noble.

"What sort of souvenir do you think would be good?"

"Souvenirs…? You just arrived, but you're already plotting to leave?"

"If it's okay for me to go, then I'm outta here."

"A little girl, you said? Did the couple running the place you're renting have a child?"

"No, she's mine."

Gregor froze, but Dale didn't realize it in the least. His thoughts were solely on the vision of Latina's smile.

"She's a great kid, and she's just way, way, waaaaaaay too cute. And she's super admirable, too. She's bravely watching the place back home right now. She told me to 'Take care' as she waved her tiny little hand. I feel like I'm gonna cry just remembering it. Ugh, I wanna hurry on back to her. Is she lonely right now? What'll I do if I've made her cry? Plus, she's still growing. She's learning new things each and every day. Will she learn to do even more things while I'm gone? What should I do? It's utter torture, missing out on Latina growing up. Yeah, I'm heading back. I'll leave right now. Hey, Gregor, what's the job this time around? Let's head out right away. I can leave if I wipe everything out immediately, yeah?"

"What the hell's happened to you?"

Gregor's reaction was totally natural, after all. The last time he'd seen Dale, he wasn't like *this*. Just what in the world had happened to bring him to such a deplorable state? The cause seemed to be the child who had come up all throughout the current conversation. Just where had she come from?

When Gregor carelessly asked those questions, he lost any chance he had of stopping his friend from gleefully talking away. He was completely bewildered and hadn't the slightest idea as to how he should react.

And just when would he stop bragging about his kid?

"So… you took in a devil child with one horn?"

After he'd heard the story of how Dale adopted Latina and all the details of what had happened up until now, Gregor had lost track of just how many times the word "cute" had been used. Although he realized early in the conversation that it was prudent to just take the whole thing in stride, he had a dumbfounded look on his face as he listened to the unexpected tale. But Dale didn't seem to be paying attention to his listener's reaction. As he was now, discussing Latina's cuteness to his heart's content was a matter of great importance.

"I'd like to have you meet Latina, too, but… I couldn't handle it if the royal family found out how cute she is and set their sights on her. Yeah. There's no way, then. If you want to meet her, then you've gotta come to our place. Think about it," said Dale arrogantly while he completely fawned over the girl.

Who the hell are you? muttered Gregor mentally, wondering who to blame for his friend's change.

"Even though we tried investigating Latina with the Akhdar's Message Board, we couldn't find any information about her. Devil villages don't interact with the outside much, and I guess that's the sort of place she came from… It's real likely that she doesn't have a single relative left to look for her."

"Well, not much is known about devil culture, after all."

"I couldn't find anything on her father's body that'd hint at where they were from, so I can't go looking for her home village. The 'crime' that got her branded with a broken horn must've been something out of her control. But that's no reason for someone from a different race like me to neglect her."

Gregor understood that reasoning. What he *didn't* understand was Dale's transformation. Just how strongly had that devil girl tugged at his heartstrings?

"Even if Latina's a devil, it's not like she sees everyone else as enemies. There's no problem with us living together."

"No problem, huh…? In that case, I suppose she doesn't know that you've slaughtered members of her race, yes?" Gregor whispered. Dale sat in silence for a while.

"…I've cut down humans for work, too. It hasn't just been devils."

"Well, that's true."

That's what it meant to live by the sword. Magical beasts weren't the only things that hurt people. It certainly wasn't rare for human nations to clash with other races, and out of all those races, devils had the deepest ties with the demon lords.

Across the world there were seven demon lords, and they were ranked as "First Demon Lord," "Second Demon Lord," and so on. Their abilities and the way they ran things varied, but they all had one thing in common: all demon lords had horns, just like devils.

Furthermore, all demon lords led a household of "demons." No one was born a demon. Instead, they became one upon entering a demon lord's house and gaining power far exceeding what they would naturally possess. And those demons were not necessarily just "people." They also included mythical beasts—beings that possessed high intelligence despite being considered animals.

But it was without a doubt the devils that made up the vast majority of the demons, and for that reason, demon lords were also called the "Kings of the Devils."

"We've confirmed the presence of someone who appears to be a subordinate of the Seventh Demon Lord."

"A demon, you mean? Or just a plain old servant?" Their power would vary greatly depending on if they were a demon or not. In fact, the difference in the threat they represented couldn't even be compared.

"I still don't know for certain. That's why I called for you," Gregor said, meeting Dale's gaze.

"I'll tag along," Dale said with a sigh.

"If you're there, then I guess it'll be fine…"

They were so deeply confident in each other's skills that they each trusted the other to watch their back.

Dale stood up. The time for his audience with the duke was drawing near. Going in his usual leather coat would be inappropriate for such an event, so he needed to put on a more proper outfit. That was why he'd stopped here before heading to meet the duke in his office at the palace. It wasn't just so he could have this chat with his friend.

"At any rate, be sure to keep yourself together and act a bit more dignified in front of my father."

"I know, I know." Dale waved and headed for the room that had been prepared for him.

This time, the young man who exited the Eldstedt family carriage was clad all in black. It was clear from the wild feel to him that he was no noble, and despite his age, he had the aura of a warrior who'd lived through many battles. When the palace guards realized who he was, they stood up straight. The glance he gave the soldier who bowed and stepped forward to guide him was incredibly cool and composed as well. This was a first-rate warrior, who without question wielded his magic and blade mercilessly. He was a prospective hero who was even now achieving great things, and might one day become a legend.

That was the sort of man he was rumored to be, and from the impression that he gave, that was no exaggeration.

While feeling the somewhat jealous gazes of the soldiers, Gregor felt conflicted—somehow relieved and somehow not—seeing the "usual" Dale next to him.

This was the man named Dale Reki.

When someone first met him, they'd say he was charming and calm, but if they were to meet him on the field of battle, they'd find a cool-headed, yet unforgiving warrior.

It was said that perhaps the young Dale had needed to become that way in order to succeed at such work. The best way to calmly deal with what he saw was to kill off his own emotions. That was how he seemed to the soldier who guided him through the palace with his back still perfectly straight.

After all, to Dale, this palace was yet another battlefield.

†

In Kreuz, several days after Dale left for the capital:

It was readily apparent that Latina was miserable. Rather than just feeling down, she was full-on wallowing in sorrow. It was like her whole body was screaming out that she was lonely.

"Latina... are you alright?" No matter how Kenneth looked at it, she clearly wasn't, but he couldn't think of anything else to say to her.

"Latina's alright... She's holding down the fort, after all," Latina responded as she sat quietly next to Kenneth while he was doing his usual preparations. Her voice sounded like it was about to vanish.

She was always like that. Even though Latina's expression and body language told otherwise, her response was that of an anxious honor student.

Kenneth let out a sigh and looked at her. "Yeah, that's right. You're holding down the fort. And Dale will definitely come back, because you're waiting for him."

Latina looked up at Kenneth and tilted her head a little, and Kenneth responded with a smile. If an adult like him looked glum too, then that would only make Latina more uneasy.

"Before you came, Dale just saw this as a place to leave his things. But now it's a 'home' for him to return to." Kenneth knew Dale very well. After all, Kenneth was the one who had taught him the basics of being an adventurer back when Dale was still a mere boy who'd only just left his village. Kenneth had brought him into his party and freely taught him everything from traveling basics to how to accept jobs, as well as all sorts of techniques for dealing with magical beasts. As his guide, Kenneth knew how much having a "big bro" to rely on could help give strength to someone setting out on their own, without any friends to support them.

"Dale always tells you 'I'm home,' right, Latina? That's proof that this is home for him now."

"Dale always tells Latina 'I'm home'?"

"That's right. But he never said that before you came. You're someone very special to him."

Dale most likely thought of Kenneth's place like a bird would think of a tree where it could rest its wings, but that didn't even come close to how important a "home" was. To Dale, this girl was that important. And so, as his "big bro," it was up to Kenneth to protect her while he was away.

"Latina is special to Dale?"

"Yeah, you are."

Latina's expression was strained, like she was just barely holding back her tears, and she tightly gripped her skirt above her knees.

"Kenneth…"

"What is it?"

"Is it alright for Latina to stay with Dale forever…?"

"If you disappeared, then Dale would run around frantically looking for you."

"Frantically?" questioned Latina, tilting her head upon hearing a word she didn't know.

"It means he'd be desperately worried."

Latina searched for words again.

"Latina… she got driven out of where she was born because she was bad. Even though Latina was the only one they threw out, Rag went with her, and then he died."

Kenneth continued on with his work nonchalantly, trying his hardest to make sure she didn't see him falter. She really did understand that she was exiled from her village, after all.

"Who was Rag?"

"Latina's parent. He was sick, but he went with Latina. Only Latina's family said she wasn't bad. When Rag died, Latina thought that she really was a bad girl, after all," said Latina, once more casting her gaze downwards. "Dale was the first who said Latina was a good girl… He was the first to say it who wasn't her family." And in a tiny voice, like she was telling him a secret, she continued, "Dale is special to Latina, too."

"…Is that so?" said Kenneth, feeling that he was a terribly pathetic adult, since he was unable to come up with any sort of decent response. Just how much had this little girl locked away in her tiny body?

"Why didn't you tell Dale any of this stuff about yourself, Latina?" He'd heard that when Dale asked her before, she hadn't seemed like she wanted to talk. So why was she opening up to Kenneth like this?

In response to his question, Latina said, "If Dale knew Latina was bad, he'd hate her. Latina's... scared of Dale hating her..."

"I see. So you couldn't talk to Dale *because* he's so important to you, huh?" said Kenneth, and Latina nodded. Even though Dale had already guessed what she had just told him, he wanted this young girl to stay by his side.

However, Latina didn't know that, and she was even scared of him knowing and wanted to hide it desperately.

Still, Latina ended up talking to me about herself like this... Just what would happen if Dale found out...?

He'd be a real pain, and it certainly wouldn't be fun to see. Dale really needed to learn from this girl's concern for others, even if only just a bit.

"Hey, Latina, do you want to try learning something before Dale gets back?"

"...Learning?"

Kenneth suddenly suggested this because he was worried that otherwise, she'd just stay depressed and wilting away until Dale returned. It would be better to give her something else to focus on. Of course, the greatest possible motivation for Latina was Dale.

"Dale's definitely going to be starving when he comes back. It takes a while to make it from the capital to Kreuz, after all. You said that you wanted to learn how to make a meal for him, right? This is a good opportunity, so I'll help you practice. Dale'll be totally shocked and happy when he hears that you made it."

"...Latina can do it?"

"It'd still be a bit much for you to do everything, but there are parts that you can handle. How about it? Wanna give it a try?"

Seeing Latina brighten up a bit, Kenneth felt relieved to the bottom of his heart. For better or worse, it was clear that Dale was immensely important to this little girl.

"Latina wants to do it. Kenneth, please teach Latina."

Even though he wasn't that doting idiot Dale, he still wanted to do something for this girl after hearing her say "please." She was just too cute.

†

Not long afterwards:

"Here, it's a shepherd's pie. I'll give you a discount, so eat it."

"So you've finally started using high-pressure sales techniques here, huh?"

Kenneth stood dauntingly before the bearded adventurer who was a regular, holding a plate with an item he hadn't ordered. He remained unshaken, even with the regular's astonished response.

"And why is it so misshapen? And aren't the insides leaking out?"

"Hey, she's still practicing. It's to be expected."

"Practicing?" repeated the bearded adventurer, who then realized who'd be "practicing" in this shop. There was only one possibility, after all. Only one little girl lived at this inn, so… "The little lady made it, huh?"

"Right, it's a work in progress from Latina."

"Alright, then. Leave it here."

Such exchanges occurred many times over the course of that day.

After thinking about what Latina could currently handle, Kenneth ended up settling on having her make a shepherd's pie. In order to have her improve as quickly as possible, it was best to have her make as many as possible. There was a limit to how many meals they needed for lodgers, but this shop was also a gathering place for men who were unrefined and didn't fuss over things like how beautifully their meals were plated, so it made for the perfect testing ground.

Shepherd's pie is a dish made by spreading mashed potatoes on top of a meat sauce and then baking it. Though it has pie in its name, it uses no pie crust, nor is it a pastry.

Latina's job was to make the mashed potatoes, spread them on a plate with the meat sauce Kenneth made, and finally, sprinkle cheese on top. Kenneth put it into and took it out of the oven, but Latina kept track of how long it baked with a serious look on her face.

Since Kenneth was the one who made the meat sauce, which was the main flavor, there weren't any huge failures. But still, the results were slightly awkward at the start, with sauce dripping out the sides, or the potatoes coming out lumpy. But as the days went by, Latina continued to improve.

After the first day, the regulars all readied themselves to help with Latina's practice without a single word from Kenneth. After all, this dish came with the bonus of a tiny waitress carrying it out. Latina had wanted to help wait the tables for a while now, but the Ocelot had customers pay their bill when they got their food, so it wasn't like they could have a young girl like her handle it. But this shepherd's pie campaign was limited to just the regulars. This meant it only involved people who were trusted enough to settle their bills at the end, so Latina was able to do the job without needing to handle the money.

As a result, the Dancing Ocelot underwent an unprecedented shepherd's pie boom.

"Thanks for waiting!"

It certainly wasn't a bad thing to see Latina enthusiastically give this her all, especially considering how she'd been hanging her head in sadness since Dale left. Whenever she was feeling lonely, an aura of depression hung over the Dancing Ocelot.

There was a rather nice-looking shepherd's pie on top of the tray that Latina was carefully carrying out. It was still just a little bit sloppy, but it would be no problem to serve it on the menu at this point.

"It's hot, so be careful, please."

—This young girl may have waited on customers more politely than anyone else at this shop.

Take your time, said the regulars in unison deep in their hearts, as Latina wore a smile on her face and hugged the now-empty tray.

The gruff men who made up the regulars were clearly perplexed at first as to how they should interact with a young girl like Latina, who would shoot even them a lovely smile. Normally a child would break out in tears if they came into contact with people like them, so they'd never really had such a charming girl smile at them the way that Latina did.

Occasionally, she'd come across someone foolish enough to act rudely towards her, perhaps because they were in a bad mood. When it came to adventurers, guys like that would be considered less than second-rate. But Latina's big eyes would just go wide in surprise, and she'd distance herself from them. Then she'd observe them from far away, like she'd found some sort of large, strange creature.

"Welcome! Thanks for waiting!"

Latina's special shepherd's pie was in great demand at the Dancing Ocelot again today.

†

Nearly half a month after Dale had departed from Kreuz, a shout of "I can finally leave!" rang out through the Eldstedt residence.

"I'm leaving right now! Get a flying dragon here ASAP! Latina's waiting for me!"

"For the time being, you at least need to still attend this evening's party. It's part of your job…"

"I don't waaaaaanna! I wanna go hooooome!"

"You need to look over the souvenir list the maids prepared, do you not? It's full of things that have been popular in the capital as of late, but it means nothing if you don't choose one yourself, yes?"

"That's right! Will Latina be happy, I wonder?"

Dale's expression shifted suddenly and completely, but Gregor wasn't particularly surprised. Over the past half a month, he'd grown used to it. In fact, he'd come to accept all sorts of things, since he'd had no choice but to do so.

During this half a month, an elite group that included Dale and Gregor had headed into the mountains on the outskirts of Ausblick in order to take down members of the Seventh Demon Lord's household. It was only just the other day that they had completed their mission and returned to the capital.

The work that Dale primarily received from Duke Eldstedt, which were jobs involving a contract from the country of Laband, involved fighting against demon lords and their households.

There was a reason only an elite few were sent on such jobs. By primarily employing adventurers, the country could avoid having to mobilize the army. If Laband used its armed forces, it would be like a declaration of war on the demon lord. The powers of a demon lord were vast, and with their household alongside them, they possessed enough strength to prove a threat to a nation on their own. If a country were to oppose them in an official capacity, a demon lord would choose to fight back alongside his house.

The seven demon lords were all independent, and they wouldn't choose to form alliances. But even so, war with a single demon lord was more than enough to shake an entire nation down to its core.

In order to hold back the threat of a demon lord with the least amount of risk, it was best to use a small group of unspecified alliance to launch a surprise attack. In other words: assassination.

Gregor was part of a ducal household, but because he wasn't officially in the employ of the military and was at least partly thought of as an adventurer publicly at this point, the mission had come his way.

When Dale arrived from Kreuz half a month ago and after they'd finished their preparations, Dale and Gregor had headed to their destination alongside the others who were to join them on this mission. All of the members of the party were adventurers who were known to possess extraordinary skills. In addition, because they were being directly contracted by the nation of Laband, they were considered every bit as trustworthy as they were skilled. They were no saints, but at the very least there were no worries about any of them becoming a traitor and stabbing their allies in the back. A reconnaissance party from the army disguised as adventurers accompanied them as well.

When they at last arrived at a forest deep in the mountains, they were able to confirm that several dragons had made a nest there, just as the scouts had reported. As it was a land awash in the blessing of

Ahmar, Ausblick was a geothermal hotspot and also an area dragons frequently used during breeding season.

"…Those are definitely dragons that serve the Seventh Demon Lord."

Especially fond of war and mayhem, the Seventh Demon Lord liked to employ dragons as a symbol of his great power. Devils had a high number of those with an affinity for Center magic, including tamers who could manipulate dragons as if they were an extension of themselves.

By confirming those dragons were targets, they also confirmed the presence of a tamer. There was one woman in a black robe, as well as a number of warriors. Each and every one of them had horns on their heads. Devil warrior helmets were specially made, so as not to conceal the horns that they were so proud of; while they covered the wearer's head, their horns remained on full display. The most dangerous one in the group, though, was the robed woman.

"…There's no mistaking it. That woman's a demon," Dale quietly warned his allies. Knowing his skill, they immediately accepted what he'd said rather than bothering with unnecessary questions.

From there on out, they didn't bother with any pointless conversation. As a group that had taken on dangerous missions together numerous times, they had naturally prepared a number of hand signals in advance.

It was Dale's magic that kicked off the battle.

"Oh earth and the spirits dwelling within you, by my name of Dale Reki I order you, shift your form according to my wishes, and swallow up all around you. 《Ground Transfiguration》"

The mana called forth by this chant vastly eclipsed that of a basic spell. A thunderous roar filled the air, and the ground beneath his target collapsed. The demon woman and warriors realized the attack was coming in time to get out of the way, but the heavy dragons were caught up in the thick of it. If Dale were a normal magic user, it wouldn't have been strange for this attack to exhaust him completely, but he didn't show even a hint of fatigue. In fact, he had smoothly unsheathed his blade, and cut his way into the midst of his confused enemies.

With that signal, Gregor, holding a scarlet Eastern longsword in his grasp, leaped into action as well. The blade had been enhanced with magic to strengthen its sharpness, and the shine coming off of it danced through the air. When it came to pure sword technique, Gregor was on a whole other level compared to Dale.

"Oh earth, by my name, I order you to strike my foes. 《Stone Spears》" In the instant that all attention had gathered on Gregor, Dale chanted this close-range attack spell. This sort of coordination was only possible because they both knew intimately how the other fought.

Sharp spears made of stone rose from the ground with such precision that it was hard to believe that this spell was the result of such a simple chant. Having been thrown off-balance, the devil warriors were then cut down by Gregor.

"Protect me!" yelled the demon woman, scolding her underlings. Pushing through the rubble, a dragon came forward to defend her. Shortly afterwards, fireballs came flying and hit the dragon in its head, scattering a great deal of heat through the surroundings.

But that wasn't the end of the magical assault. Next up, an electrical shock came running across the ground. At this point, the woman's primary goal would be to stop this wave of attacks coming from multiple magic users.

The demon woman nervously realized that the soldiers under her command had been defeated so quickly by just two humans, and the rest of her dragons were still in the depths of that unbelievably deep hole. The one by her side now had only managed to crawl out by climbing over its brethren. She wouldn't get the rest of them back so easily.

"Kill them!" she yelled, having no other options left. Even though she knew it was a poor move, the woman gave that order to the sole underling she had left. Her plan was to buy the time needed to escape on her own.

She ordered the dragon to create an escape route in the magic users' blind spot... or at least, that was her intention. But before she knew it, the warrior in the black leather coat was closing in on her. Her eyes opened wide in surprise as she saw her dragon stopped by the other adventurers.

The woman was shocked to realize that this man had been aiming for her alone from the very start. It was the unfaltering move of a man who had absolute faith that his allies could handle a dragon without him.

Even so, the woman pulled out a dagger in an instant, and swung it down at Dale in a blow far quicker than that of the warriors. Dale didn't falter in the slightest, stopping her attack with his left arm. A dull, metallic sound resounded from his gauntlet, and the knife slid across its surface without leaving so much as a scratch. Without even stopping to look at the despair in the woman's eyes, Dale slashed his sword to the side.

That was how it went. Both in tense situations and in battle, Dale did nothing that would shame his reputation as a first-rate adventurer. There were no issues with the way he handled his work, either. But in between all of that...

"Maaaaan, I have a serious Latina deficiency! Latinaaaaaaaaa!"

"...What is it that you're lacking?"

"Latina, I said. I've had way too little Latina lately…." Dale said in a strange voice as he suddenly flailed.

"I wanna see Latina… How is she doing…?" he asked when he was gazing up at the sky, tears streaming down his face.

"Latina…" he muttered when he was stirring a campfire.

To sum it up, he was emotionally unstable.

The others grew distant from him as a result. After all, these attacks generally came as fits, and anyone who was dragged into them found it nothing but uncomfortable.

He was just blowing off steam, or at least that's what Gregor decided, choosing the most favorable explanation possible for his friend's actions. That was his small bit of pity towards the poor man.

And now, Gregor's greatest task was to stop Dale before he amassed a mountain of souvenirs so huge that it would be too much for a flying dragon to carry.

†

"Latina!!" Dale screamed out in joy as he flung open the door to the Dancing Ocelot. In his other hand he held his luggage, which had clearly increased since when he'd left.

"*That's* the first thing that comes out of your mouth?" Rita responded, disgusted that that was all he'd have to say upon seeing her for the first time in half a month. He'd clearly gotten worse in that span of time, in pretty much every way.

"Oh, it's you, Rita. Where's Latina?"

"Latina's with Kenneth," she answered.

Just then, apparently hearing the ruckus, the person in question suddenly poked her tiny head out from inside the shop. Latina broke out in a brilliant smile and came running to his side.

"Dale, welcome back!!"

Compared to how she'd looked half a month prior, Latina had filled back out to a size closer to an average child, and now she appeared even more adorable than Dale remembered.

"I'm home, Latina! You did a great job holding down the fort. Were you lonely? I'm so sorry. I was super lonely, too!"

"Latina was lonely, but she's happy that you made it home safely. Welcome back!" Latina said with a smile as Dale hugged her tight.

"Ah, you really do bring me solace, Latina…" Dale muttered in response, awash in a flood of emotions.

I gave it my all, and it was so very worth it.

"Actually, Latina, I got you souvenirs…"

"Hold on, Dale."

Dale had been excitedly preparing to give her the souvenirs, only for Latina to now quickly push away, leaving him in shock. As he saw her hurry with fast, little footsteps to Kenneth in the kitchen, his face showed that he was clearly stricken with grief. His eyes lost all focus, and he hollowly murmured, "H-Half a month was too long, huh…? Hehehe… If I wipe all the demons from the face of the earth, then maybe I won't need to leave her ever again…"

"You seem pretty worn out." Realizing that he was showing this much fatigue even when he was indulging in his eccentricities, Rita couldn't help but sympathize. "Latina really did give it her all. I told her she could stay with us in our room 'til you got back, thinking she'd feel too lonely if she was in that attic all by herself. But she just said, 'Latina wants to stay in Dale's room.' She said she was fine sleeping alone too, because 'Dale's scent makes Latina feel relaxed.'"

"Latina was alright? Everything went fine?"

"Well, she did seem lonely. Still, she had something to strive towards, so she managed to more or less pull herself together."

As Rita told him about how Latina had been and what had happened in Kreuz while he was away, the little girl returned from the kitchen. In her hands she firmly held a tray, on top of which there was a piping-hot shepherd's pie and a brightly colored, jiggling gelatin desert filled with cut-up fruit.

"Dale, Latina made this. She worked hard so you could eat it."

"Y-You made it, Latina?"

"She gave it her all."

As Dale's trembling hands took the tray from Latina, who had a proud smile on her face, he was overcome with emotion.

"I can't eat it! That'd be such a waste!" he yelled.

"No, you've gotta eat it." Rita's comebacks remained firm even after half a month.

"By the way, Dale, we figured out something important while you were away."

"Huh?"

Kenneth suddenly cut into the conversation just as Dale was in the midst of enjoying the fruits of Latina's hard work, with the girl herself seated smiling on his lap. Ignoring Dale's reaction, Kenneth continued.

"Just the other day, Latina's friend Chloe told Latina that they were going to school starting this fall, and asked if she'd come, too."

"What?"

"Chloe, and Marcel, and all of them are going, because they're the same age," said Latina, looking up at Dale from his lap. Looking back at her, he thought back on her friends. He'd figured they were a bit older than Latina and thought of the young girl as someone to dote on.

"She asked if Latina wants to go too, because she's also the same age."

119

It took Dale a bit of time to digest those words.

"…What?"

"Apparently, it's true," said Kenneth with a nod as Dale looked towards him for an explanation.

"Latina, your birthday's next month, right?" asked Dale.

"Yeah."

"Is that right? I'll need get some presents ready, then!"

"Go ahead and tell Dale how old you'll be," said Kenneth encouragingly.

"Hmm? Latina will be eight," she replied, tilting her head as if to say she didn't know why she was being asked.

For a moment, Dale was frozen stiff and at a loss for words. Seeing that reaction, Kenneth nodded his head.

"…So you're seven right now, Latina?" continued Kenneth.

"Hmm? Yes, Latina is seven."

"You're so little, Latina…" Dale commented.

Kenneth agreed. "Yeah, she is."

"Latina is little?"

All of the adults had thought she was five or six. Latina was just that small. Still, now that Dale thought about it, Latina's words and actions had been surprisingly sharp, considering the age they'd thought she was. The way she spoke made her seem young, but she had only just picked up the language, so it was a result of a lack of grammar and vocabulary skills.

She'd be eight soon. When children were that young, age differences of a year or two had a huge effect.

The adults realized that they'd been wrong due to their own preconceptions.

"Is she growing slower because she's a devil?" Dale asked.

"I thought that too, and tried asking the regulars, but apparently devil kids grow at roughly the same rate as human children. Everything slows down once they reach maturity, and they spend a long time as adults."

"Latina… is little?"

"You're just small," commented Dale.

"Hmm?"

Seemingly truly confused by the adults all looking at her so seriously, Latina once more tilted her head.

5: The Little Girl's Everyday Life, Full of Friends and Magic

Even just from seeing her skip along, it was obvious that the young girl was enjoying herself. Her beautiful platinum hair, which was tied up in brilliant blue ribbons, swayed side to side along with her movements, occasionally shining in the light. She seemed to have grown quite fond of her light-blue plaid dress as of late, and sure enough, she picked it out of the small white wicker basket to wear again today.

Her expression brightened further when she saw her friends playing in the plaza.

"Chloe!" yelled Latina, vigorously waving and running towards the girl.

The southern district of Kreuz, where Latina lived, was both a rougher neighborhood where commoners lived, as well as a location for shops that served adventurers and travelers. For the most part, it wasn't a suitable place for children to play. There were affordable inns that served people with no questions asked, as well as bars where adventurers who failed to get work would drink themselves into a stupor from the middle of the day on, and even shops that stank of cheap perfumes used to satisfy the desires of men. Those were the sorts of businesses that surrounded the Dancing Ocelot.

As a result, Latina was only allowed to go out alone on the southern district's main street and the path from the Dancing Ocelot that led there. Fortunately, the Dancing Ocelot was positioned close to the center of the southern district. There were a great number of shops aimed at adventurers and travelers near the entrance to town, and stores that offered lower prices in exchange for lower quality were especially prevalent. The Dancing Ocelot's owners chose its location to separate itself from all that.

Until just recently, Latina had been forbidden from going out alone, but since she was old enough that she'd be going to school soon, there was a limit to how much longer that ban could last. This was something she'd absolutely need to get used to as she grew older.

There was a plaza in the center of town, and lately, one of Latina's favorite things was meeting there with her friends from the eastern district and playing together. There was usually a market at the center of the plaza, so although the area was good for walking around and looking at goods, it wasn't a suitable place to play.

There was a park a short distance away, so that was where the children headed. The townsfolk also used it as a place to relax. As Kreuz was a city, it was, of course, rather lacking in greenery, so even though the park was a man-made mix of grass, trees, and flowerbeds, it was always full of people enjoying a stroll, or the shouts of children having fun.

There were quite a few children playing in the plaza that Latina didn't recognize. As she slipped past them and found her way to her friends, she lit up in a brilliant smile.

"What's up, Latina? You look happy."

"Did something good happen?"

In response to Chloe and Marcel's questions, Latina happily reported, "Dale came back!"

"That so?"

"Good for you, Latina."

Latina's friends had seen how deeply depressed she was when her dad was away. These were honest words of congratulations at seeing their tiny friend finally able to smile from the depths of her heart again.

"Dale said these are souvenirs for everyone. Wanna have a snack?"

Latina smiled and held out a basket packed with sweets. Rudy realized it was food and stared gleefully at it, which made Anthony give a sarcastic laugh.

"Wow, those look expensive! Can I eat all of them?"

"Watch out, Latina. Rudy really will gobble them all down if you let him."

These four were Latina's primary playmates. The one who stood at the head of the group and acted as leader was the only girl, Chloe. She and Latina already got along well enough to be called best friends. For Latina, Chloe was someone she respected. She firmly and resolutely held the position of power even amongst a group of boys, so Latina found her to be truly amazing. And Chloe, in turn, thought of Latina as a smart girl who knew many things that she didn't. Each saw the other as their equal, as someone who had what they lacked. That was why they were able to become so close so quickly, despite their entirely different personalities. Or perhaps it should be said that those differences were what actually drew them to one another. Rather than feeling jealous, they respected one another instead.

Latina had also quickly grown close to the boy known as Marcel, who had a gentle personality and a round face that was just a tad on the plump side. As he was always kind to Latina and was careful not to frighten her, he was the girl's second favorite, after Chloe.

If asked about the slender, brown-haired boy named Anthony, Latina would say that she didn't know him all that well. But it at least seemed that she didn't dislike him. He was the sort of kid that Chloe would call shrewd, while adults would say he had his head on straight.

And then finally, there was the tallest boy in the group. Latina wasn't overly fond of Rudy (his real name was Rudolf, but his friends called him by this nickname). Their first meeting had left a poor impression, and even afterwards, he kept picking on the devil girl and playing tricks on her. This was always followed by a harsh counterattack from Chloe, but he showed no sign of learning his lesson whatsoever. Having not had much interaction with kids her own age, Latina didn't quite know how to deal with Rudy, who was easily the most childish one in the group.

Having been born and raised in Kreuz, the four children were well known around town, so as long as Latina was following after them, she was easily accepted, even into groups of kids she'd never met. And so, Latina was able to play together with friends for the first time ever.

"What should we play today?"

"We were gonna play a game of octopus tag."

"It'll be with those kids over there. You wanna come along too, Latina?"

"Yeah!"

The four taught Latina how to play. It was a variant on normal tag where you'd join hands with whoever was "it" when they caught you, and then chase after the others together. It was best enjoyed as a large group.

With Latina having joined them, the group of five rushed over to where the other children were playing in the park.

It was a sign of Kreuz's prosperity and wholesome nature that children were able to run about while joyfully shouting like this in its streets. There was nothing to really endanger the children here in the middle of the day, despite the heavy flow of travelers through town. Part of that was because the plaza was near the lord's manor, where the local government was run.

Kreuz did have slums, though to be precise they were actually outside the walls and clustered up against them. There were children in the town itself who lived rather poorly as well, being forced to work from a young age, but even so, the overwhelming majority of children there were able to have fun, play, and just enjoy their childhood, perhaps more so than any other town in Laband.

After playing numerous games of octopus tag and running around to the point of exhaustion, the children naturally dispersed. After saying goodbye to the other kids, Latina and her friends sat down off to the side in the grass, where they pulled out the contents of the basket. After such hearty exercise, they'd worked up quite an appetite, so it was time for a snack.

The brownies wrapped in thin paper looked truly tasty, but as Latina handed them out to her friends, she didn't look at all like someone excited to dig into some sweets. She had her cheeks puffed out, showing her displeasure. She was trying her hardest to show how she felt, but instead it made her look like a cute little animal.

"Cheer up, Latina."

"These sweets are delicious."

Anthony and Marcel tried to cheer Latina up with comments like that as they devoured their snacks. And yet, Latina's puffed-up cheeks did not deflate.

"Why did Rudy always go after Latina?" she asked unhappily.

"Hmm? Because you're so small and slow."

Completely unmoved by Latina's complaints, Rudy kept wolfing down the brownies he was holding in each hand.

These were high-class goods from famous shops frequented by the nobles of the capital, but to the children, the only thing that mattered was that they were rich and delicious sweets.

"There were kids smaller than Latina."

"But even if they were littler, they were still faster than you."

"Latina isn't slow!" said Latina, her cheeks swelling up like balloons again. She was clearly displeased; Rudy had greatly injured her pride.

"It's because Rudy always chases after Latina the most!" Latina asserted, causing Anthony to laugh awkwardly, while Chloe knitted her brows. Marcel casually threw in a "That's right" as well. It was hard to gauge what Marcel's reaction meant, but Rudy himself remained indifferent, and unwrapped yet another brownie.

"Isn't it weird that he doesn't notice it himself?" whispered Chloe.

"Rudy's still a kid, after all," Anthony replied, whispering as well.

They may have still been young, but Rudy's actions were easy to see right through. In fact, they were almost embarrassed to see their old friend act so blatantly.

The other topic of this conversation, Latina, bit into a brownie as well, and her expression suddenly brightened, as if she no longer cared about Rudy at all.

Ever since their first meeting, Chloe and the others saw Latina as someone special. The girl had brilliant, sparkling platinum hair and wore beautiful ribbons the likes of which commoner children could only hope to wear for festivals. At first, she had been all skin and bones, but now that she had filled back out, she was incredibly cute and charming. She was like a princess from a fairytale. She was born in a far-off nation, so the way she spoke was a little awkward, but she could use magic. She had no birth parents, but she lived with her adoptive father in a shop where adventurers gathered. Any one of these aspects would seem extraordinary to the children, and *all* of them were true of Latina.

All four of the children also knew about her horns. In fact, it was Latina herself who had shown them the little black horn hidden behind her ribbon. Latina had even let Chloe touch it, and she thought it felt smooth to the touch, with a faint bit of warmth to it. From the sad look on Latina's face, the children could tell that they shouldn't ask about her broken left horn. Even Rudy, who seemed to be entirely lacking in tact, understood that much.

With a sort of flexibility that adults lacked, the children easily accepted that devils were slightly different from them, but they were still people.

At first they had indeed been drawn to how unique she was, but now their tiny, loveable friend Latina was someone very precious to them. And because she knew that, they were very precious to Latina as well.

†

Her friends had known that Latina could use magic since they first met her, but Dale hadn't. To start with, he never would've guessed that it was even possible for a kid that young in the first place. He never even considered it.

When the topic happened to come up during dinner, he was so surprised that he unconsciously dropped his fork.

"Huh? You can use magic, Latina?"

"Yeah. But only one basic healing spell."

Ever since this conversation, Dale had been left wondering whether or not he should give her proper magic training. In particular, he was worried about attack magic.

Hmm… attack magic is dangerous, but I also kind of want to have her learn it for self-defense…

The only thing that he'd worried over more was her broken horn. After all, she was such a cute little girl. He couldn't help but be concerned that some people with ill intentions would set their sights on her at some point. As long as she had the power to use magic, then he should teach her the skills she'd need to protect herself.

Knowing Latina, it's not like she'd use it carelessly and end up hurting someone...

Thus, he arrived at the decision to teach her magic, even knowing the risk it posed as a weapon.

On a different day, in the early afternoon:

Dale pulled out the textbook he'd once used to learn magic, and he called for Latina.

"Latina, what element is the recovery magic you can use?"

"Umm... shining."

"'Holy,' huh...? Well then, do you know if you have opposing or adjacent elements?"

"No, Latina doesn't know."

As Latina shook her head, Dale started pondering.

The ability to use mana to cause all sorts of phenomena was called magic. The amount varied, but the power source known as mana existed in all things. Because of that, someone not having mana at all was extremely unlikely. But when it came to magic, that was a different story entirely. To start with, you could only use magic corresponding to the elements you had an affinity for.

There were seven elements: Holy, Water, Earth, Dark, Fire, Wind, and finally Center.

The categories of affinities were referred to as "lone Center," "opposing dyad," and "adjacent triad." As the names would imply, outside of those who could only utilize Center magic, people either possessed two attributes that were opposite, or three with a high level of compatibility for one another.

In Dale's case, he had affinity for Water, Earth, and Dark.

"Well then, we'll have to look into that first…"

What affinities you could use had a large effect on the magic you could employ. Take healing magic, for example. That only fell under the elements of Holy, Water, and Earth, and couldn't be used without such an affinity. And even if they all had healing magic, Water healing was most effective on external wounds and ailments. Earth healing, meanwhile, had the greatest effect in terms of recovering stamina and healing heavy injuries. And lastly, Holy healing was all-purpose, able to deal with any condition, meaning they all had their own strong points.

"Oh water," said Dale, in a chant too short to even count as a spell. In response, a faint bit of mana flickered over the palm of his hand.

"Ooh…"

"Do you get it? If you get a mana response when you call out to an element like I did just now, then that means you have that affinity. You're a devil, so the spell language shouldn't be any problem for you…"

"Hmm? What do you mean?" asked Latina with her head tilted, puzzled.

"Ah," murmured Dale, and he continued on with his explanation. "The other races refer to devils like you as 'natural-born magic users.' That's because the language of the devils uses the same words as the language used in magic spells. To be honest, most people have no aptitude for it. They aren't even able to manage the pronunciation. 'People who can use magic' are essentially the same as 'people who can manipulate spell language'… Is that too confusing?"

"Hmm… So Latina can use magic because she can speak it?"

"Right, that applies to all devils."

Dale took Latina's hand and had her call out to the elements. As a result of going through this process, they discovered that she had an aptitude for Holy and Dark.

"Since you can already use healing magic, you probably already know this, but a spell is created by choosing an element, declaring your mastery over it, and defining the phenomenon that will occur. And then finally, you finish it off with the spell name."

"Huh…?"

From her reaction, it appeared that though she could use magic, she may not have studied the theory behind it. That was understandable, though, because normally it'd be unthinkable for such a young girl to use magic in the first place. Dale didn't know if it was "normal" for devils, though.

"When you learned that healing magic, how were you taught it?"

"Latina remembered the whole thing. And she was taught how to use mana."

"Brute memorization, huh? Could you show me your healing magic, Latina?"

"Yeah," Latina answered, with a look of serious concentration. She chanted the spell so smoothly it was almost like she was reciting poetry.

"Oh light of heaven, grant this request by my name, and please heal those who have been wounded. 《Healing Light》"

Seeing the overflowing gentle light, Dale breathed a sigh of relief.

"That's a wonderful spell. Even without any sort of tool, you still had proper control over it."

"Really? Latina did good?"

"Yeah. That was amazing, Latina," said Dale as he picked up the textbook. He flipped through the pages, his gaze darting back and forth until he at last found what he was looking for.

"Well, let's put off learning the theory behind it for the time being... How about we try having you memorize some simple Dark spells, as well as Holy and Dark composite magic?"

Since she was a devil, making it her mother tongue, Latina was of course well versed in the spell language. Though Dale was supposed to be the one doing the teaching, he ended up asking her about vocabulary he didn't recognize.

"Spells are a language, after all. Naturally, if you stretch them out and add more words, it'll result in a stronger magic. But in exchange, you'll expend more mana and it'll be harder to control."

"Really?"

"Yeah. For example, with that 《Healing Light》 spell you just used, a simpler version would be something like 'Oh heavens, by my name, I order you to heal these wounds. 《Healing Light》,' and that would still activate. That'd be plenty to deal with scratches and things, and it'd use up a lot less mana."

"So if Latina made it even longer, it could heal big injuries?"

"It'd be hard to manage, but... I think you could manage it with a tool."

Magic users made use of tools like staffs and rings to help them control their spells. By exercising minute control, they could set the amount of mana that was consumed, allowing them to achieve the greatest possible efficiency.

There did exist powerful attack magic that could obliterate a wide area, and in theory, it was possible to execute a spell that could reduce an entire army to ashes in a single blow. But in exchange, that would require a massive amount of mana, as well as the skill to control it, plus an incredibly verbose chant. It simply wasn't practical. If you thought of it as reciting an entire epic on the field of battle, it was easy to imagine just how unrealistic it was to execute.

The fundamental role for spellcasters was to launch a large number of basic spells to attack or support the front line with the appropriate magic for the situation while safely staying in the rear.

"But Dale, Latina had never even seen magical devices before."

"Devils are an insular lot, so they don't have much interaction with other races. And we humans don't know much at all about devil customs and the like," Dale started, before continuing on. "Magical devices are tools made to allow people to manipulate mana, even if they can't use magic, and can be used regardless of affinities. And the ability to make those magical devices, which is to say the power to 'enchant,' is the special trait of us humans."

Just like devils could all use magic, each race had its own unique trait. The angels had wings on their backs to fly through the sky, and the scale-covered merfolk were able to breathe underwater. Both of those were racial traits. Humans didn't have any notable physical traits, but were able to create and use tools.

Even outside of the seven races of man, there were those who were able to create large phenomena that exceeded mere 'magic,' thanks in large part to their species' traits. It was for this reason that even large magical beasts such as dragons could fly through the sky. There was no such thing as a spell that could make you fly, after all. It was said that such beings held racial traits that let them rule the heavens.

"They're a product of humans, so they wouldn't show up in places that don't trade. That's just how it is."

"But they're so handy. Why don't devils get along with everyone else?"

"...Yeah, I wonder why." Dale knew one of the reasons for that, but he'd never dare to say it.

There was a trend when it came to insular peoples.

—Dale would later come to regret not bringing this up.

†

Latina was born in the sixth month.

As there were seven central gods who ruled over the world, a great many things were also expressed in seven parts. Therefore, a year was split up according to that rule of seven. In other words, the time that it took for the seasons to make a full rotation was split up into a multiple of seven, with there being 14 months to a year. Days were also divided into 14 parts, which were named after shortened versions of the gods' names, such as the hour of Mar and the hour of Saj. Typically, the day hours were referred to as "front," whereas the night hours were called "back." Dawn was "the front hour of Mar," sunset was "the back hour of Mar," the evening was "the front hour of Saj," and the time before dawn was "the back hour of Saj."

To prepare for Latina's birth month, Dale put in a request to Chloe's parents.

In this world, they hadn't established the use of birth certificates, so "birthdays" in particular were often uncertain. So though there was a custom of celebrating births, it was done in terms of months instead.

Chloe's parents were tailors. They may have been subcontractors who didn't own their own shop, but they were definitely skilled. And so, Dale made an order from their store on the main street, requesting them in particular.

Latina was interested in how clothes were made. Apparently, she wanted to see her clothes being sewn, so after asking Chloe if it was alright, she hurried on over to watch. That's how Latina learned the basics of needlework. Dale hadn't meant for Latina to impose so much on Chloe's family, so he hurried over with a gift to show his gratitude, somewhat flustered.

However, Chloe's mother said with a smile, "When she's with Latina, Chloe tries her hardest to show how good she is. She's always had some talent, but she gave up on things quickly and didn't try to practice at all. I'm the one who should be thanking *you*."

What Dale had tailored was a light-pink dress with flower embroidery. When it was at last finished, summer was quickly approaching in the town of Kreuz.

"Oh dark and shadows, grant my wishes by my name, draw away the heat and lower the temperature. 《Temperature reduction》"

With a small crackling sound, the contents of the bowl in front of Latina froze. After making sure, she started to mix the ingredients with a spatula. Creating ice required Dark and Water combination magic, so Latina couldn't handle that, as she didn't have the necessary affinities. But it was possible to lower the temperature of something and freeze it using the Dark element alone. After all, in many ways the Dark element covered the ability to make things drop, whereas the Holy element caused things to rise.

Dale had revised spells so they'd be easier to use and had taught them to Latina, so she was now able to use magic in her everyday life. Since summer was coming, Latina tried making some of the frozen sweets that she loved. With the ingredients to make things like sherbet and ice cream at the ready, she made something different each and every day. She learned the recipes from Kenneth, of course. It took some time when he made them because he needed to use magical devices, but because Latina was able to use magic, she could do it far more quickly.

It could be said that this sort of cooking was suited to magic users, but it wasn't like Kenneth could put out a request for one to help him with this.

After freezing and mixing countless times, Latina had at last finished making a soft and fluffy sherbet, and she excitedly carried it into the shop.

"Rita, thanks for working so hard. Take a break, okay?"

"Thanks, Latina."

Rita was tackling all sorts of papers at her normal spot behind the counter, and was seemingly exhausted from the heat. Even though the windows and doors were left wide open, the breeze wasn't necessarily always blowing through, and with the sort of men who frequented the shop, just looking around made it feel that much hotter. It was rough even on Rita, who'd been involved with this line of work in some form or another ever since she was born.

When she took a bite of the dessert that Latina had carefully prepared, an expression of pure bliss washed over her.

"Ahhh… it's delicious. Even if I ask Kenneth for it, he only makes it every now and again. Thanks, Latina. It really is tasty."

"You're very welcome." As Latina dug into her own portion, she broke out in a smile. "But it's tastier when Kenneth makes it. Latina wonders why."

"It's because he doesn't want to lose to you, Latina," responded Rita with a chuckle when she saw Latina's somewhat dissatisfied expression.

"Kenneth's trying hard, too?"

"Hmm?"

Latina seemed somewhat puzzled by Rita's words, but before the young girl had come to the shop, Kenneth had hardly ever made sweets. Rita knew full well that her husband was working hard to develop new recipes for Latina, so much so that his repertoire was large enough that he could open a confectionery shop. He kept a cool and composed expression, but he never slacked for even a single day in order to remain a target of the girl's admiration. Rita certainly didn't dislike seeing her husband turn his childish desire to not lose into a chance to improve himself like this.

"You sure aren't a picky eater, are you, Latina? Are spicy foods a little rough for you, though?"

"When Latina eats something spicy, it makes her mouth feel…" She puffed up her cheeks and blew in and out, like she was trying to cool down her mouth. "But when it's just got pepper on it, Latina can handle it," she said, looking over at the salt and pepper shakers on the other side of the counter.

When Dale had ordered a dish with some spice to it once, it had caught Latina's interest, but even a single bite proved far too much for her. Her face turned red, and she chugged down her cup of water in a single go, and yet that still wasn't enough, so she'd darted to the kitchen at full speed for a refill. But apparently, she was so flustered at the time that she didn't think to grab something to put it in before activating the magical device. When the adults came after her, they'd found her flailing about in front of the flowing water.

They'd felt bad for her, but they couldn't help but laugh.

"What's your favorite, Latina? Egg dishes, perhaps?"

"Latina likes eggs, especially when they're all fluffy. And she likes cheese and cream sauce, too."

When she first came to the shop, Kenneth often made her lots of egg dishes, which had plenty of nutrients and were easy to eat. Apparently, that had had a big impact on her.

"Bread's good when it's all soft and fluffy, but omelets are even tastier."

Even now, French toast was one of her breakfast staples.

"What sort of foods did you eat back in your home village, Latina?"

"Hmm? ***, and ******."

Perhaps because she didn't possess the appropriate vocabulary, Latina used words from the devil language instead.

"Umm… what did they taste like?"

"Well… they didn't have much flavor. Latina only ever ate that, so Kenneth's meals really surprised her. He makes all sorts of things, and they're all tasty."

Latina broke out in a wide smile, not even realizing that Rita was at a loss for words.

"So Latina wants to learn how to make tasty meals too, since they make people happy."

†

"Every year I end up wondering if I'm an idiot, wearing a long black coat this time of year," Dale grumbled, completely exhausted after returning from a day's work exterminating magical beasts.

"Try saying that in front of someone in full platemail," Kenneth chided, all the while filling a glass with cold water.

Dale's coat was imbued with magic, so on top of being far lighter than a suit of armor, it also offered an exemplary amount of defense. When paired with his stab-resistant tunic, his equipment provided more than enough protection.

But even so, it was awfully hot in the summer. Incredibly, terribly hot.

"Dale, welcome home. It's cold, so eat up."

"I'm back, Latina. Thanks."

Though he'd clearly been in a bad mood up until then, Dale abruptly broke out in a smile. Latina had brought out her frozen dessert on top of a tray.

"You've been making this sort of stuff a lot, Latina. You're not using too much magic and tiring yourself out, right?"

Mana consumption wasn't something that was visible to the naked eye, but you could recognize it by feelings of exhaustion and fatigue. If you overused your magic, you'd lose the concentration required to manipulate mana in the first place. It could even cause you to faint, so it was especially important to keep your mana expenditure limit in mind on the field of battle.

And so, Dale asked that question while taking the bowl from Latina, and she in turn gave a nod.

"Latina is fine. She's done it a lot, and she learned how to do it for just a small area."

"…I see."

Seeing Dale stare at Latina with a more serious look on his face than normal, Kenneth grew suspicious.

"What is it, Dale?"

"Well… I was wondering if all devils were so good at controlling mana. It looks like Latina's already mastered designating an area of effect."

"…Is it really that impressive?"

Kenneth had purely been a warrior, so he didn't know anything about using magic.

"She's just a kid, and she hasn't studied the theory behind it. And yet through practice alone, she's managed to narrow down an area of effect for her magic, and she's optimizing the balance between mana usage and power. I may have taught her that it could be done, but I didn't teach her *how* to do it…"

Kenneth took a long, hard look at Latina, and she glanced back in confusion.

Dale continued. "And with spells, she's been applying the sort of subtle techniques from the healing magic she already knew, rather than the simple sort I taught her. Normally, the burden of controlling it should increase alongside that."

"Latina learned because Dale taught her. Before, she used a lot of mana at once. Now, she just uses what she needs. It's a lot easier now."

"…See?"

"Right. Latina really may be a genius. She learns everything so quickly, after all."

"Is that so?" replied Dale, causing Kenneth to look at him as if to say, "You're just realizing this now?"

"Yeah, with cooking and cleaning, and even needlework lately. Even if you just teach it to her once, Latina understands it amazingly quickly. It's stranger to me that she was apparently raised in an environment that left her unable to do such things 'til now, when she's such a sharp kid."

"Huh?"

"I mean, think about it. She's such a quick learner, so why does it seem that nobody taught her about magic and housework until now? She's so clever that it wouldn't surprise me to see her learn stuff without even being taught. Even if we're talking about different races, that's just too big of a discrepancy."

When she first came to the shop, Latina at least knew how to take care of herself. But even so, there were a great number of things that she couldn't do. Kenneth had to carefully teach her how to do things like hold a knife and wring out a washcloth from scratch. He couldn't imagine that the devils' lifestyle was *that* different.

"Right…" was all Dale was able to say in response, realizing how true those words were.

Seeing the adults staring at her, Latina tilted her head, just as she always did.

"What is it?"

"So it was an environment where you weren't taught anything, or one where you didn't need to do anything, huh…?"

"Hmm? You mean Latina?"

"Yeah. Did anyone teach you anything like we've done back where you were born?"

"Hmm… Latina still wasn't decided."

At this somewhat indecipherable response from Latina, this time the adults tilted their heads.

"What 'wasn't decided'?"

"Latina doesn't really know either, but Li… No, Latina doesn't know anything."

She almost said something, but covered her mouth with her hands and shook her head.

Both Kenneth and Dale realized at this point that Latina wouldn't disclose anything else. Despite appearances, she was quite stubborn, after all.

If you asked him why he'd gone to check on her, Kenneth would find it hard to come up with an answer. Primarily, he'd become concerned when he saw how horribly pale she looked. That's why he caught the small, strange noise, though he normally would've missed it.

Back then, Dale hadn't brought up a certain fact that he'd realized. This was because he didn't want to hurt Latina. But put another way, that meant that he realized full well that this knowledge would hurt her. As her guardian... as her parent, he shouldn't have turned a blind eye.

Latina was an incredibly clever girl. However, she was also still very young. Her way of thinking and emotions still hadn't grown enough to match that cleverness.

There was a sign.

The best thing would've been if he could've stopped this ahead of time.

It was just a little, but things were definitely starting to move... And even though it was only a tiny bit, this incident would definitely help shape her fate.

†

Autumn was fast approaching in Kreuz.

Latina and her friends had started attending school at the temple of Asfar in the center of town. Asfar was the god that presided over education; in a town of Kreuz's size, there were temples all over, and they shouldered the task of providing children with the necessary amount of teaching.

In the case of Kreuz, children received two years of education, starting in the fall of the year that they turned eight. When the statistics only covered those who lived in towns, the literacy rate in Laband wasn't half bad.

In towns, information flowed in the form of writing for not just merchants, but everyone. And so, reading was an important skill for blue-collar workers and adventurers as well.

"Does something have you feeling down, Latina?"

"No, Latina is fine. She's alright."

Seeing Latina look somehow depressed as she prepared to go to school, Dale grew concerned. However, Latina's expression suddenly shifted, and she forced a smile.

When she first started going to school, she seemed like she was truly having fun each and every day. She appeared to enjoy learning new things, and she'd excitedly report those things back to Dale. But for the last few days, there had been a strange change.

As Dale hugged Latina tight, there was a mystified expression on her face.

"Did something change at school lately?"

Latina's small body suddenly twitched a little in surprise.

"…We got a new lady teacher," replied Latina in a quiet voice, with her face towards the ground.

"Did something happen with her?"

"No. Everyone says the old teacher made learning more fun, that's all."

Dale knitted his brows. Considering how Latina was acting, he didn't believe that that was the extent of the situation at all. But with how stubborn she was, it wouldn't be easy to get her to speak up.

"Latina, it's not a bad thing to let someone help you out. You really are important to me, so how about relying on me a bit?"

"Dale... Latina is fine. She's just... a little scared of the teacher."

Dale would later come to regret that he hadn't taken greater heed at the time. He should've thought more on what "scary" was to Latina, who didn't stop smiling or even feel timid when she interacted with the ruffians known as adventurers as she lived at the Dancing Ocelot.

After a few more days, Latina looked even more depressed. She told Dale each day how much fun she had with her friends, and how she'd made new friends as well. But not once did Latina bring up her teacher.

The adults figured she may have been trying to avoid thinking about the matter.

One day, Latina returned looking ghastly pale, in a truly awful state. It was so bad that when Kenneth went to greet her like he always did, his voice caught in his throat. She looked so unwell that it wouldn't have been a surprise if she collapsed at any moment; her clothes and hair were disheveled, and one of her ribbons was coming untied. But more than all of that, it was the expression on her face that pierced Kenneth's heart.

Latina seemed to be in a daze, and looked like she had lost everything precious to her. Her expression was one of utter despair.

Ever since Kenneth had met the young girl, she'd shown him plenty of smiles.

Even though she'd lost her father, the only person she could rely on, in that forest, she'd survived on her own. Those were sad, painful, harsh memories that would be too much for even an adult to handle, much less a child. And yet, Latina still smiled.

In that moment, Kenneth felt that he was seeing the soft and gentle fragments Latina had hidden in the depths of her heart coming to the surface.

"Latina, did something happen…?"

Latina responded by trembling greatly in shock and looking like she was about to break out in tears.

But even so, she forced out a response of, "It's… nothing," before turning around and heading towards the stairs.

If it were Dale, he would have scooped her up in a hug without saying a word and completely pampered her until she felt completely at ease, mind and soul. He'd put off the reason for why she was hurt for later, and focus first on smothering her in affection. That's definitely what would have happened, had Dale not been out for work. If he had been the one to greet Latina instead of Kenneth, things may have ended differently.

Not much time had passed before Kenneth heard a strange sound from overhead. It was a dull sound of the sort he'd never heard before. The air seemed to vibrate heavily. The sound was enough to give him a truly ominous feeling.

Acting on reflex alone, Kenneth ran up the stairs and climbed up into the attic.

There, he found Latina collapsed on the floor.

With only the light coming in through the window, the room was dim.

For a moment, he was unable to tell what had happened to her.

But when he took a step closer, Kenneth realized Latina's head was resting in a pool of blood. Her platinum hair was dyed scarlet.

"Latina!"

The reason that Kenneth was so disturbed, despite having grown used to seeing such injuries in his previous occupation, was because Latina was the only one in the room. In other words, she had done this to herself.

Kenneth picked her up and hurried down the stairs, all the while pushing a clean cloth from Dale's room up against her wound. In no time at all, the cloth turned red. Just applying pressure wasn't enough to stop the flow of blood.

Kenneth could only think about getting healing magic cast on her as quickly as possible, or perhaps cauterizing the wound.

Latina had broken off her remaining horn.

Blood vessels and nerves both passed through devils' horns, and though they looked quite tough at first glance, they were sensitive organs. If they were damaged, then it would result in intense pain and a heavy flow of blood.

The unconscious Latina remained limp, not moving an inch.

Kenneth ran into the Dancing Ocelot's storefront, holding Latina in his arms. His grim expression shocked Rita, as well as the regulars engaged in idle chatter.

"Kenneth, what—"

"Is there anyone here who can use healing magic?!"

It was hard to say whether they realized what his cry meant or spotted the blood-soaked girl in his arms first.

"Latina?!"

"The little lady's hurt?!"

Rita let out a scream, and unfitting to her usual, strong-willed personality, the color completely drained from her face.

The bearded regular stood up from his chair with a crash, and pushed one of the men who had come along with him forward. The middle-aged man rushed over to Kenneth and pointed the palm of his hand towards Latina's head.

"My magic can't do all that much."

"I don't care. Just stop the bleeding, please!"

As the healing spell was cast, the flow of blood didn't stop, but it did at least slow.

In the meantime, Kenneth headed over to Rita.

"Just to be safe, I'm gonna take her to the clinic at the temple of Niili. Tell Dale what's going on when he comes back. And we'll shut down the shop for the day."

"G-Got it. Kenneth… what happened to Latina?"

"I'm not sure of the details myself. For now, I've got to get her treated first. I'm off!"

Holding Latina in his arms once more, Kenneth sprinted to the temple of Niili as fast as he could.

This is something they'd come to know later:

Latina had the ability to vaguely sense when something would do her harm. That was why she had been able to survive all alone in the forest. It was why she was able to find only things that were okay to eat, when there were so many poisonous plants and animals all around. And it was why she knew to hide when beasts that would harm her were prowling nearby.

When she first met Dale, she sensed that he wouldn't hurt her.

Able to sense all of this unconsciously, Latina could sense her "enemies" on instinct.

And that instinct had been functioning properly this time as well.

†

It was three days after the incident that Dale headed for the temple of Asfar.

Rather than his usual leather coat and tunic, it was a high-class black robe that he wore, which was another sort of "battle armor" for him. The sigil hanging from his neck was also not part of his usual attire.

The rather elaborate, complex design of the sigil displayed his status at the shrine. It wasn't just to show that he had been granted divine protection. After all, there were strict regulations regarding what sort of materials you could use to make such a sigil, and those regulations were based on your position in the temple. Just from looking at him, it was obvious that Dale held a high position there. The elderly priestess who ran the temple of Asfar in Kreuz was also aware of him.

Dale was an adventurer with deep ties to the duke serving as the current prime minister. However, temples were recognized as extraterritorial organizations, entirely detached from a nation's authority. Even though the temple was in the nation of Laband, it had no need to listen to orders from the royal family or the duke.

It was difficult to say how true that was in practice, but that was, at least, the official stance.

Dale knew all of that full well, which was precisely why he visited the temple of Asfar not as an adventurer serving under a ducal family, but as someone who held the rank of a high priest.

Normally, he wasn't fond of letting people know that he possessed divine protection. After all, it's not like he'd asked to be born that way.

The divine protection that Dale possessed was a miraculous power that was granted by the gods to fragile mortals. And so, no temples could treat one who possessed such power poorly, even if it came from a god other than the one they served. The gods all stood as equals, after all.

Furthermore, Dale's divine protection happened to be especially strong. It's not as though the strength of divine protection was directly tied to status, but as those who served the awe-inspiring gods, the people of the temple couldn't help but stand in awe of individuals who possessed a power that served as proof of their favor with the gods themselves. Additionally, there was no such thing as a priest who couldn't recognize the strength of someone's divine protection, and aside from those of such low rank that they were hired just to take care of chores and the like, everyone who served at a temple possessed some amount of it.

Temples originally started out as institutions built to offer a sanctuary that would grant protection to those who possessed the unusual power known as divine protection. Therefore, only those who possessed divine power were permitted to take up the post of priest.

"I don't think there's any need for me to repeat my reason for coming here. I believe I have the right to inquire into just what happened."

"Yes, that's certainly true."

As the top priestess of the temple, she had heard a report. The devil girl who had been adopted by the young man before her had started coming to the school managed by the temple this fall. The priestess also heard what the teacher had shamefully done to the child.

"Normally, no matter what principles or position someone may hold, I wouldn't try to fight them on it. And it's not like 'mankind supremacists' are all that rare. But I still think that at least when it comes to the citizens of Kreuz, that'd be considered quite a narrow-minded point of view."

"…It's just as you say."

"In a town like this, built on the backs of travelers and trade, no matter what your occupation, you're bound to have had plenty of interaction with other races. It's hard to imagine that someone serving the god of education would fail to know something so obvious."

On the surface, Dale didn't show any anger. But this was a man who could make you feel a bottomless sense of dread, even when his face remained perfectly calm. Even though they were meeting for the first time, the priestess felt a cold sweat run down her back. Even as a high-ranking priestess, it wasn't often that she encountered someone with the drive to slaughter massive monsters and magical beasts.

"I hear that she called her out in front of the children and mocked her for being part of another race while abusively spouting her own baseless opinions. Is that the opinion of Asfar nowadays?"

"She was born near the land of the devils, and… she lost her family in a quarrel with them, so…"

"So it's alright to mock an innocent girl and treat her like a monster? Is that the temple's excuse? How novel."

153

"No, of course not…"

While wiping the sweat from her brow, the priestess searched for what to say. With what he had said, it was clear that the man before her eyes knew the whole story of what had happened.

Dale hadn't spent the three days before he came here just idling about. Of course he was worried about Latina's condition and didn't want to leave her side. But at the same time, he also felt the need to look into just what had happened to her.

He didn't stop at just asking Latina's friends. He also asked for the help of Rita, who was an expert at gathering information, and even checked with people like Chloe's mother to hear the rumors about town. By comparing and scrutinizing the information he gathered, he at last had the evidence he needed. From there, he rather precisely deduced the chain of events. Dale gave the impression of being overly emotional when it came to Latina, but it was precisely because he was so furious that he was able to remain focused. If he couldn't do that, then he wouldn't be worthy of being called "first-rate."

Apparently, this was how the incident went:

It seemed that the priestess who had become Latina's new teacher had just transferred from a town in a neighboring country.

The children described her as someone who always spoke in a shrill voice. That may not have been her intention, but children were sensitive to such things, and didn't try to sugarcoat their words.

Apparently, Latina kept her distance from this priestess from the very start. She'd thought quite well of the previous teacher, and she had never acted towards someone else like she did the new priestess. Her friends were wary as well, it seemed.

And then that day came.

The priestess realized Latina had horns.

"A devil…" she muttered under her breath, and grabbed Latina's hair. As the smooth horn hidden behind her ribbon was exposed, the priestess spat out hatefully, "What is such a detestable *thing* doing in a town for people?!" as if that was an obvious question.

As Latina was shocked and at a loss for words, the woman's venomous words kept flowing. "There's no way that such beasts that live for over a hundred years without their appearance changing in the least could be called 'people,' is there?"

The priestess loudly proclaimed all of this to the bewildered children, looking absolutely confident in what she had said.

With Latina's hair still in her grasp and the young girl unable to move, the priestess thrust Latina forward, as if showing off prey she had caught.

"These subhumans who aren't part of humankind aren't 'people.' These grotesque monsters make a mockery of how people should live. Don't be fooled, everyone!"

The population of humankind was far greater than that of the other races. As a result, there were many who held incredibly insular thoughts exceeding those of the so-called "insular races." In that regard, the priestess was "just" spouting off her own principles.

But in this town, that was heresy.

Not even realizing the disgust the children were feeling, she continued to rant.

"And devils in particular are evil and cowardly beasts, with close ties to the demon lords themselves! You mustn't ever let your guard down. The way she's hidden what she is to slip into this town should be more proof than anything else!"

"Aah!" cried out Latina, her face ghastly pale as the woman gripped her hair even tighter. That served as a signal for her friends to leap into action.

Chloe threw her lithograph (a black stone each student used for taking notes) as hard as she could. It didn't actually hit the priestess, but it did smash against the wall with a loud crash.

"What are you doing?! That's dangerous!"

Distracted by Chloe's actions, the priestess's grasp loosened, and Latina fell to the floor.

After exchanging glances, Anthony and Marcel moved to save their friend.

At that moment, Rudy kicked his desk. It was meant for three children, so it only shook a bit with his force alone, but it was more than enough to catch the woman's attention.

"Stop that! What in the world are you doing?!"

As she yelled out, the children in the classroom's disgust started to turn into fear.

They looked up and saw that woman screaming in her shrill voice while their good friend cowered, looking like she was about to break out in tears. To the children, it was abundantly clear who the real monster was here.

When Rudy went to kick the desk again, Chloe kicked the other end at the same time. This time, the sound was massive, and it collapsed to the floor.

"Stop! Stop!"

Having gotten the hang of it, the pair toppled one desk after another, causing the woman's shrill voice to ring out even louder. Several of the kids started crying.

The woman screamed out, seemingly irritated even by their weeping. "Stop! Stop!! Stooooop!!"

Drawn by the abnormal cacophony, the other priests came running to see what was happening. What they found was sobbing, frightened children in a classroom that looked like it had been hit by a storm. And shouting the center of all that was their 'colleague,' a look like an ogre on her face, and a group of children glaring back at her, standing to protect a girl who looked white as a sheet.

The other priests rushed into the classroom and forced out the so-called teacher, who was still carrying on with her unsightly rant.

"Teacher..." called out a sickly-looking Latina to one of the priests, who had been their teacher until just recently, as he was leading the woman away. "What's different? Is Latina... are devils different from everyone else?"

"Latina, that's..."

"How does Latina live differently? What did she mean, that she'll live for 100 years? ...Is Latina different from everyone else?"

Unable to lie in response to her grief-filled words, the priest frowned sadly. Taking a knee, he looked Latina in the eye.

"...The biggest difference between humans and devils can't be seen by the naked eye. Devils are especially long-lived, and several times as long as humans."

Latina's grey eyes opened wide. She was a smart enough child to understand what that meant.

She headed back home, unable to hide her shock. Even the voices of her concerned friends didn't seem to reach her.

And so, she broke off her horn using her own magic.

Latina had already received treatment by the time Dale made it home and heard about the incident.

Niili was the god who ruled over life and death, so Niili's temples served as organizations for the research of things like pathology, medical technology, and pharmaceuticals. The townsfolk general used the temples as clinics, where the results of that research were applied.

Kenneth had brought Latina to such a clinic.

Fortunately, she wasn't in serious condition, due in part to the fact that she was found so quickly, as well as the excellent first aid she received.

Even though devils were a rather robust race, Latina was still young, so if her tiny body lost too much blood, she wouldn't have been able to recover.

When Dale came running to the clinic, he found Latina resting in bed, her face pale from blood loss. She had regained consciousness, but her eyes looked somehow vacant and lifeless as she slowly stirred upon noticing that someone had arrived. Those grey eyes quivered when they saw him standing there in a daze, breathing heavily.

"Dale…" she called out in a slow, hoarse voice.

Feeling relieved at hearing Latina call his name, he sat down on the edge of the bed and bent over.

"Latina… why…?" he whispered in a quivering voice as he reached out and touched her cheek.

With this, her expression broke down.

"U-uh… uwuh…" blubbered Latina incomprehensively. Tears rolled down her face.

"Latina… does it hurt?" Dale asked anxiously, but he got no response. She just kept weeping and gripping Dale's hand tightly.

She shook her head back and forth.

"Latina doesn't need it… she doesn't need it…" Dale heard her cry out amongst her sobs.

"Latina?"

"Latina doesn't need the proof that she's a devil… She wishes she never had any horns!"

Still not knowing what had happened to her, Dale was at a loss. But seeing the state she was in, he knew that he shouldn't carelessly reprimand her.

"Latina… Latina. What is it? What happened?"

"Latina hates it. Why… why is Latina a devil? She doesn't live where devils are…. and they said they don't want her. Everyone who cares about Latina, who said she could stay with them, are all humans…"

This was the first time he'd ever seen Latina this upset.

"Why is Latina the only one who lives longer? Latina doesn't want to be the only one left… after everyone else dies…" Latina shouted her feelings and worries that she'd hidden from Dale up 'til now, her voice filled with grief, and the words reverberated throughout the room.

With that cry, Dale realized what Latina had been worrying about. She'd realized that devils and humans were born with different amounts of time, or lifespans.

"Latina hates it… She hates it… Why, why…? Latina wishes she wasn't a devil… She wants to be the same as everyone else… She never wants to be all alone… the only one left, ever again… Latina wants to stay with Dale and her friends forever… She doesn't want to be all alone again, with everyone gone…"

What had hurt Latina the most and driven her to this despair wasn't someone's malice. It was truth… the truth of the immutable differences between the races.

That truth was what Dale had been unable to tell Latina before. What the more insular races all had in common was that they were long-lived. Different lifespans in turn led to a great difference in what someone felt was valuable. For example, ten years felt quite different for humans than it did for devils. And with that absolutely different sense of value, it was difficult to meet one another halfway.

"Latina, I'm sorry…"

It may not have made sense to apologize, but in that instant, those were the words that came from his mouth.

Dale picked up the sobbing Latina, and he hugged her tight. Her soft hair rested against his cheek, and he gently brushed his finger along her wound, which still had some faint traces of blood around it.

"It must've hurt… I'm so sorry, Latina…"

As she grieved and cried with all her might, seemingly even finding it difficult to breathe, Dale awkwardly yet tenderly stroked her back, trying to take away at least a little of the girl's pain.

†

It was later on that Dale learned what had happened to Latina.

He had put off telling her about the differences between races, and in turn it had been thrust in front of her with the worst possible timing. She had injured herself using the attack magic that he had taught her. With her exceptional level of control, she was able to concentrate on one spot and successfully break off her horn, whereas before she wouldn't have had enough power to do so. That was a fact.

And that was why he was so angry; he was frustrated with himself as well.

With such thoughts on his mind, Dale stared straight at the middle-aged priestess, who was wiping the sweat from her brow.

He broke out in a smile that even he found cold.

"According to the rumors, that teacher apparently caused a similar incident in her previous town, yeah?"

The priestess's face grew paler and paler.

No one in Kreuz should have had that information, so it was no surprise that she was shocked that he knew.

Just what sort of man had she made an enemy of? She needed to keep that question in mind. In addition to being an expert at gathering information, Dale had the authority to demand more than just intel. Even without using his connection to the duke, he could apply pressure that a single priestess could not hope to fight against.

"She caused the same sort of trouble with an elf, right? And that was in a town with deep trade connections to the elves, with a tourist industry centered around their songs. Apparently, that incident led to elves refusing to perform in public, correct?"

That was why she'd been hurriedly moved to the far-off town of Kreuz. She couldn't stay in that town any longer.

This unexpected change of personnel led to great confusion in Kreuz's temple of Asfar as well. That was why Latina's teacher had been swapped out so suddenly. In order to suppress the chaos in the other town, one of the high-ranking priests from Kreuz had been sent there, and to fill the hole he left, Latina's previous teacher was moved into his role.

The people working at the shrine didn't imagine that she would possibly be foolish enough to do the same thing again right after having been moved for having caused so much trouble. And yet, the woman herself completely believed that her principles weren't mistaken, and she had no intention of reflecting on her mistakes. After all, the people blaming her were in the wrong, or so she thought.

"By the authority of my divine protection, I demand arbitration."

"That's…"

Hearing Dale's dignified words, the priestess's heart skipped a beat. His request was the right of any high-ranking priest, and could be demanded even of the followers of other gods. This was the primary reason that he'd come here today as an official priest and wearing a sigil.

"It's not as though I don't understand the desire to protect members of your organization, but if you intend to protect someone who's guilty of this much, then I expect you've resolved yourself to face equally harsh repercussions."

With a sharp gaze to drive in the point, Dale continued. "If you're unwilling to accept my request, then I'm ready to take my demand to the temple of Ahmar. And if that happens, then your culpability will come into question as well, seeing how you stayed quiet despite knowing of the prior incident."

In addition to being the god of war, Ahmar also presided over arbitration and judgment. His temples served to pass down rulings that exceeded the authority and laws of any land. There, they handed down merciless and impartial judgments. To the guilty, that was effectively the same as a death sentence.

If she didn't want a great number of those at the temple to be punished for their joint responsibility, she needed to cast out the culprit and make her take responsibility for her actions. That was the meaning behind Dale's demand.

Dale had said something to Latina as he tightly held the sobbing girl in the clinic. He spoke the words that he wanted and needed to say, that he couldn't avoid, as her father.

"But Latina, even if we were both humans, I'd definitely die first. I'm older, and it wouldn't be odd for me to die at any time in my line of work…"

At these unwanted words, Latina began wriggling fiercely. She shook her head back and forth, as if saying she didn't want to accept them, and she'd cried out so strongly that it sounded like a shriek. As she cried out with all her might that she hated that, Dale held her tight, so she couldn't just run away from what he was saying.

"But Latina, listen closely. I'm really, truly glad to have met you. Even if our time together is limited, I'm glad to spend it with you." Dale was as loud as possible so he wouldn't be drowned out by her cries as he said what he needed to.

Ever since he'd met her, his life had changed greatly. And he was truly grateful for that. It was undoubtedly this small girl in his arms who gave him such gentle, precious moments, and let him be himself.

"I'm glad I met you, Latina. I'll never regret that. So please, Latina, don't say that you would've been better off if we'd never met…"

Latina looked up at Dale with tears still streaming down her face. She tried to respond, but her voice just wouldn't come. Sobbing heavily, she shook her head in a different way than she had before.

"N-No... L-Latina..."

While coughing and wheezing over and over, she at last found her words.

"Latina... really is glad... that she met Dale..."

"Thank you, Latina. If the thought of parting from us makes you cry that much, then that just goes to show how important we are to you, right? That makes me happy."

"Yeah... Dale is special for Latina. That's right..."

Dale gave her a kiss on her tear-stained cheek, which surprised the young girl. But it was far better to see her surprised than sad.

Dale smiled, looking like a child who'd just pulled off a prank. He looked straight into Latina's eyes.

"I'm glad I met you, Latina. No matter when I die, I'm sure I'll still be able to say that... So until that time comes, will you stay with me?"

"Yeah. Latina's glad she met Dale..."

"I love you, Latina."

"Latina loves Dale best of all..."

Even if it was just a bit, she broke out in a smile, making him feel incredibly relieved. For that smile, he'd be able to work harder than he ever had before. That's what he thought from the bottom of his heart.

†

Thanks to the use of healing magic, the treatment of Latina's wound was finished before too long. The reason she was held at the clinic was because she was still weak from blood loss and her mental state was still unstable.

By the time Dale launched his assault on the temple of Asfar, Latina had already been discharged from the clinic. She continued her treatment and also took it easy at the Dancing Ocelot, but that was more because of the worrying adults than her own choice.

It was around that time that Chloe came to visit, and learned for the first time of what Latina had done. She'd thought that Latina had been resting due to the shock of the incident. She never would have thought that Latina had broken off her own horn, losing enough blood in the process that she could've even lost her life as well.

And as a result, a soft *smack* sound reverberated through the attic. Having been hit, Latina opened her eyes wide. And the one who had done the hitting, Chloe, had broken out in tears. Sobbing heavily, she hit her friend again.

Considering she regularly beat boys into submission, it was obvious that Chloe wasn't putting her full strength into the blows, but Latina was still shocked enough that she couldn't speak. Even if Chloe had used violence to protect Latina before, she'd never turned it on the young girl herself.

"You idiot! How could you be so dumb, Latina?! Why would you do something like that?!"

And all the while, Chloe wore a pained expression on her face.

"Your horn was so pretty! And whether you had it or not, you're still you! And…"

It was the first time Latina had ever seen Chloe cry. Seeing her strong-willed best friend, braver than any boy, look so hurt, Latina wanted to break out in tears as well.

"Latina, you could have died… you big dummy!"

Seeing Chloe raise her voice with tears running down her face, Latina at last understood. She'd made her precious friend feel that same fear, and terror, and helplessness.

"Latina's sorry... so sorry, Chloe..." said Latina, her voice cutting off midway through as she started sobbing hard as well.

Afterwards, the two held each other close and kept on crying loudly.

Hearing this, Dale turned back around and descended the stairs. He was truly grateful that Latina had a girl like that as her best friend. He may have been the most important person to Latina right now, but he'd have to work hard to maintain that position.

Dale had also heard of how Chloe acted to protect Latina before anyone else at the school. She really was quite a gallant young girl.

Having let out her emotions in front of her precious father and friend, Latina seemed completely relieved, almost like something had been exorcised from inside her.

The truth could not be changed; that was something the clever young girl understood full well, but she had been driven this far by feelings of not wanting to accept it. Now, however, Latina was able to process it, and she realized that there were people who would accept her no matter what.

"Latina is very happy," whispered the girl, letting down her hair.

Even without her ribbons, there were no longer any horns to be seen on her head. If you looked very closely, then you could see the remains of them hidden under her hair, but at a glance, it was hard to tell that she was a devil.

"When Rag died, Latina thought that she would die, too. But then Dale found her and said she could come with him, which made her so very happy. And then Rita and Kenneth were so nice, and Latina met Chloe and them, and every day became so fun… So Latina had started to forget…"

Latina rested in Dale's arms, showing no sign of the swell of emotions she'd shown the other day. She really was quite mature for her age. As Dale stroked her hair, she wore a peaceful, happy expression on her face.

"Rag taught Latina that everyone needs to part someday, when they die… Latina wanted things to stay like they were, so she was afraid of having to say goodbye."

"Everyone finds that scary. I mean, when I heard you were hurt so badly, I felt like my heart had stopped."

"Chloe cried, too. And so Latina realized how lucky she was. Chloe didn't want to say goodbye to her either, so that made Latina really happy," she said, with a smile that looked more suited to an adult on her young face. She was still quite young, but she looked truly lovely as she put all of her joy and gratitude into that smile pointed at Dale.

"Latina is glad she came to Kreuz, and that she met everyone… Latina's so happy right now, and it's all because Dale found her. Thank you, Dale!"

†

"I thought I was going to cry when Latina said that," Dale said half-braggingly as he actually drank wine that hadn't been watered down for once.

Kenneth looked a bit disgusted as he slammed down a plate of bar snacks in front of him, but he also knew just how panicked Dale had been until Latina's condition stabilized and he was able to finally calm down. Well, even Rita had been unable to keep her mind on work and had made mistakes that she normally never would, so Kenneth kept his mouth shut.

By now, Latina was already a precious fixture of the Dancing Ocelot.

"Today we're celebrating Latina getting better, so everyone can have a single drink on me!" Dale shouted out, only to get a chorus of boos in return.

"You cheapskate!"

"You should say you'll pick up the entire tab in this kind of situation, right?"

"Oh, shut it! If I said that, then you'd all drink me into bankruptcy!" Undaunted, Dale yelled back, and the bar erupted in booming laughter.

"That's for sure!"

"Rita, get everyone a glass of the best booze in the joint!"

"You mean the stuff we have set aside?" asked Rita, with a beaming smile on her face.

"Oh, so you're gonna bring out stuff you don't usually have on sale?"

"Even if they did put it out, it's too expensive to actually sell, probably."

"It's a special occasion, so let's use the biggest mugs we've got," said Kenneth.

"Kenneth?! This sort of stuff isn't usually served in a mug, right?!" Dale protested.

"What are you saying?" Kenneth shot back. "If the owner says it can be served in a mug, then it can be served in a mug."

Rita nodded. "That's right."

"What a pair!"

With this exchange, the laughs only grew louder. Amongst all the merrymaking, a troubadour started performing, which was usually banned in the shop. Of course, this performance wasn't for profit, but instead kicked off a singing contest, with the regulars joining in.

The cheerfulness only drew even more cheer, and soon the normally quiet Dancing Ocelot was engulfed in an unheard-of level of liveliness.

"What is it? Why's everyone so rowdy?" said Latina while rubbing her eyes, having been woken by the noise. For pajamas, she had on a simple lavender dress.

When the gruff men all called out her name at once, even Latina couldn't help but be startled. However, the drunken outlaws were too out of it to take that into account.

"Here's the star of the show!" they cried out, and she was carried to the center of the shop.

"What? Huh?"

Latina blinked in amazement as her confusion was met with a round of applause rather than an answer.

Even Rita, who normally would have stopped them, simply smiled as she carried out large mugs. Seeing Dale and Kenneth grinning as well, Latina remained calm, despite being surprised.

A merry melody rang through the air.

Seeing everyone around her smile, Latina started to look happy herself. After some encouragement, she gave herself over to the music on the temporary stage erected in the center of the shop.

And so on that day, a new fact came to light:

Though Latina seemed to be skilled at everything, with no weaknesses to speak of, it turned out that she utterly lacked a sense of rhythm and had no ear for music.

The Dancing Ocelot was a shop that served as a base for adventurers in Kreuz. There was a tendency for the regulars there to be overly strong-willed, and one of the biggest names in Kreuz, Sylvester Delius, was one of them.

Sylvester was a man who'd racked up quite a few exploits as an adventurer. Minstrels sang a number of songs about him, and as a result, even people in other countries heard of his achievements. But he'd spent most of his time in the country of Laband, and out of those who called themselves adventurers there, those who didn't know his name were in the overwhelming minority.

Nowadays, he took up residence in a mansion in Kreuz's western district, the high-end residential area of town. In addition to prestige, this man had also amassed a great deal of wealth, and though he was now half-retired, he still had quite a strong presence to him.

And that was why he kept a watchful eye on the Dancing Ocelot.

As a town that was hospitable towards adventurers and travelers, Kreuz also sought to have adventurers rein their own kind in. Though the restrictions may have been loose, if they allowed them to act without restraint, then the town would be driven to ruin by outlaws. Regulations, therefore, were necessary to keep Kreuz prosperous. Protecting that prosperity also meant protecting the jobs of adventurers.

One of the reasons that Rita was able to safely run the Dancing Ocelot was because there was an influential man like Sylvester there to keep the others in line. There was a reason Sylvester came there to eat nearly every meal, and drank cheap beer there every night: he was standing watch as a great number of travelers and adventurers came and went. Furthermore, he also served as an advisor for his fellow adventurers, and even now, he remained someone who was both feared and respected by a great number of those in his trade.

"Mr. Syl, here's your tea."

"Thanks, little lady," said Sylvester with a smile, taking the cup off of her tray. That smile of his, however, looked villainous enough to make most children flee in terror. His intimidating, bearded face was truly fitting for this first-rate adventurer.

"Cards?"

"Right."

"You're good at that, right, Mr. Syl?"

This young girl didn't care at all about his fame or his great deeds. She only saw him as a nice, older man who was at the shop all the time.

If you didn't know any better, he seemed to be just one of the men who would come in and drink from noon on now and again, amusing themselves with card games all the while, in an entirely undignified manner.

By the way, when Latina's friends first locked eyes with Sylvester, they'd fled out of the shop at lightning speed. But that was how regular kids reacted, whereas Latina's was outside of the norm. No matter how intimidating or villainous the customers who came to the Dancing Ocelot looked, she wasn't scared in the least.

Even now, she stood at Sylvester's side, watching over the card game as it progressed and occasionally directing a charming smile towards the players. The men all smiled right back at the young girl, even though they knew their grins were frightening enough to give children nightmares. Latina, however, just stood there looking happy. Her smiles were an extra perk at this shop, and they came for free and as often as you'd want.

†

"Mr. Syl!"

Hearing a voice that he recognized as he walked through town, Sylvester turned around. Latina was running towards him with quick little steps, waving all the while.

"What is it, little lady?"

"You forgot something in the store."

"So you came and brought it to me? Sorry about that."

"No problem at all," Latina said with a smile, handing a small leather bag to Sylvester. Her platinum hair, which was tied to the side with yellow ribbons, bobbed along with her movements.

Kenneth would've said, "Don't bother, since he'll be back soon enough," but this earnest little girl had been worried when she saw he had forgotten something and come chasing after him.

"Are you alright going back alone, little lady?" Sylvester asked, unable to hide the worry in his voice.

They were near the center of the southern district right now. This area was far seedier than where the Dancing Ocelot was.

"Latina will head straight home," Latina said with pride, pointing in the direction she'd be heading. She didn't like being treated like a little kid by the people around her.

He wasn't just worried about her getting lost, and even though he couldn't think of anything else to bring up, that was plenty enough reason to treat her like a child. Her actions were still far too cute and charming to not think of her that way.

"But…"

"Latina's fine! See you later, Mr. Syl!"

Sylvester was still concerned about her, but Latina simply waved goodbye and turned around. With her orange skirt fluttering in the wind, she headed back the same way she had come.

— Sylvester had been right to be worried.

A strong wind suddenly swept past Latina on her way back to the Dancing Ocelot.

"Ah!"

Latina managed to hold down her skirt as the gale started to lift it, but the cloud of dust it kicked up got in her eyes. She rubbed her eyes with both hands, and because of the distraction, she failed to realize that her hair had gotten messed up by the wind. She also didn't realize that one of her broken horns could be seen underneath a now-loose yellow ribbon, and that some men happened to see that, only for a wicked sneer to appear on their faces.

"Little miss."

"Hmm?"

Hearing a man's voice that she didn't recognize, Latina stopped rubbing her eyes and took a look. In a way, she was accustomed to seeing men like him, and he was shooting a friendly smile her way.

"…Are you an adventurer?"

"That's right. I've got something I want to ask you, little miss…"

"Please ask the gatekeepers or the guards," Latina firmly replied, unlike her normal, cheerful self.

"Don't say that…" said the man, moving one step closer.

That was when Latina started running.

"Damn it!"

"Don't let her get away!"

It was two different male voices that cursed at her sudden movement. Without even turning around, Latina was able to grasp at least some information about who was following her.

What should Latina do…?

Dale and Kenneth were always warning her about this, so she knew full well that devils with broken horns like her were easy targets for people with ill intentions. She brought her hand up to her head and confirmed that the ribbon had come loose. It was just as she was afraid of.

Those people… are bad.

Because she was always playing with her friends, Latina had more strength in her tiny body than one might expect from looking at her. She was able to speedily slip past the people walking down the road.

What should Latina do…? She's just getting further from the Ocelot…

Since that was the case, Latina decided to head for the walls of the city. There would be gatekeepers stationed there, and that may include some of the regulars she knew. In that case, she'd have someone to help her.

But apparently, the people chasing her guessed what she was thinking.

"…!"

As the men leaped out of nowhere in front of her, Latina suddenly changed course.

"She's a feisty one!"

"She's first-rate merchandise, so don't rough her up too much!"

What should she do…? What should she do…?

If push came to shove, then she'd have to launch a barrage of attack magic. If she hit them with precisely targeted magic, then she'd be able to stop them in their tracks. Dale had forbid her from using attack magic ever since she broke her horn, but considering the circumstances, she didn't have a choice.

Thanks to her strong decisiveness, she'd been thinking of the safest way to defeat the men from the very start. That was likely a result of the way her parents had raised her.

It was just then, however, that she saw the back of someone she recognized. She was so relieved that she almost cried.

It may have been lucky for her pursuers as well that he had appeared before she could take action.

"Mr. Syl!" Latina cried out, half in tears.

The expression on the man's face was frightening enough to make even an ogre flee in terror.

"What is it, little lady?"

"Mr. Syl, Mr. Syl…" Latina sobbed and clung tightly to Sylvester. She wasn't scared of his terrifying expression in the least, and instead looked at him with trust and relief.

From the way Latina had come running to him, out of breath, and the two men he'd never seen before chasing after her, Sylvester immediately inferred what had happened. As he sent a rage-filled glare their way, the men went pale with fear. They exchanged sly glances, and apparently decided to try to talk their way out of this.

"Well… you know, we didn't really…"

"The kid looked like she was lost, so we were just trying to get her attention."

The men had clearly failed their kidnapping. Normally, nobody would press them further on that excuse.

But they were up against the wrong opponent; they'd chosen their target poorly, as well.

Sylvester's expression didn't budge in the least. His now-tightly gripped fists were more than enough to serve as lethal weapons.

"Is that all you've got to say? Then it's time for you to die."

Even if he was practically retired at this point, Sylvester was still a legendary adventurer. So of course, having his rage directed at them, the thugs couldn't help but shudder.

They'd turned deathly pale, and their teeth started to chatter.

"What are you doing there?!" called out a commanding voice. Looking in that direction, they saw several guards coming their way. Seeing those guards, who were charged with maintaining the public order in Kreuz, the men who'd attempted the kidnapping felt relieved. A cry of *We're saved!* rang out in the depths of their hearts,

However, they were not so fortunate.

The captain of the guards saw Latina crying behind Sylvester, and immediately made his decision.

There were many guards and gatekeepers amongst the regulars at the Dancing Ocelot. It was a friendly and affordable shop, after all. More than that, it was also because those who were charged with keeping the peace needed to pay special attention to the movements of adventurers. Visiting the shops that adventurers were based out of and keeping their eyes and ears open was one of their more important duties.

On the surface, there was no tension between them, but there was most definitely a wide divide between the adventurers and the guards. But even so, nowadays they were comrades in at least one regard.

All of the regulars agreed that Dale was a doting idiot. But regardless of all that, Latina really was cute. Just seeing her toddle around the shop was soothing, and when she handed them a glass of water with a smile, they couldn't help but feel all warm and fuzzy.

The girl who sent them off with a, "Don't push yourself at work," or a, "Come again. And don't get hurt, okay?" was just plain adorable.

More or less all of the adventurers, not just Dale, had fallen for her charm, even if they were practically gangsters.

It was the same for the guards. Their job had them constantly dealing with ruffians, and it couldn't be handled without some definite skill. Because of that, they were also often feared by the townsfolk that they protected.

"Good work always going on patrol!" the young girl, who was practically a symbol of what they were protecting, would say, and that of course helped to motivate them.

Latina was undoubtedly an idol for the regulars of the Dancing Ocelot.

Her would-be kidnappers had leaped out of the frying pan and into the fire. There was no room for excuses or extenuating circumstances when it came to being judged for the grave sin of making Latina cry.

And yet, Sylvester and the guard did agree on one thing: "Better us than Dale." Which is to say, it was an act of mercy to deal with the men themselves rather than letting him get involved.

That night at the Dancing Ocelot, Latina was going around to the regulars with a big bottle of wine in her tiny arms and pouring some out for them. She went to not just Sylvester, but the guard captain as well, and stood on her tiptoes to fill their glasses.

Rather than any sort of reward or words of gratitude from Dale, they just wanted to see Latina giving her all. The result was quite a spectacle.

Kreuz, the second biggest town in Laband. There was a great force at work in this town, and it was continuing to expand even now.

Everyone in an organization has their own rank and responsibilities. Though they'd normally be antagonistic to one another, the advisor and influential figure for adventurers and the captain of the town guard were the two heads of a certain organization.

This organization, which included many other famous adventurers, and was gaining the support of young ones as well, was nicknamed the "Platinum Fairy Princess Protection Committee," as well as the "Young Girl's Bodyguards."

At some point, Latina ended up standing at the top of a powerful faction in Kreuz, possibly without Dale even realizing it.

Afterword

They say that "if the wind blows, the bucket makers prosper," but I didn't expect a case of "if you go to a field day, you become an author."

Nice to meet you, or good to see you again, to those of you who read the web version. I'm CHIROLU, and I'd like to sincerely thank you for picking up this work, *If It's for My Daughter, I'd Even Defeat a Demon Lord*.

I mentioned it at the beginning, but everything started when I encountered an application to participate in a field day as part of a tour, which could only be completed on a computer or a smart phone. In order to complete it, I finally upgraded from a flip phone, and that's how I ran into web novels, which I had avoided until then. As I indulged in reading on numerous sites, I got an itch to write my own story, and went about proving that even those of us without a computer can make submissions via a smart phone. After writing several short- and medium-length works, I got a little carried away and started my first long-form novel. Thanks to good timing and a lot of luck, a great number of people happened to see it. After a serious lecture from my former boss about how I needed to grab the reins and take charge of my life, all sorts of things happened, leading up to the release of this book. It's been almost a year since then.

I have to say that I honestly don't know how it happened.

If it weren't for that tour application, I may still be using a flip phone with a battery that died at the drop of a hat, and I imagine if I'd purchased a computer instead of a smart phone, I wouldn't have gotten so into web novels. And if you could only post stories via a computer, I wouldn't have ended up writing this work.

Looking back, I can't think of it as anything but a bundle of coincidences and random chance.

I participated in that tour in hopes of spicing up my life a bit, and though it was in a way I certainly hadn't expected, that's what happened.

To wrap up, I'd like to give my thanks to everyone who helped make this book a reality. Truffle, the titular daughter that you drew is truly cute. And above all, to those of you who chose this book out of so many options, you have my deepest gratitude.

As long as this book brought you at least a little joy, then I'll feel truly blessed.

February 2015,
CHIROLU

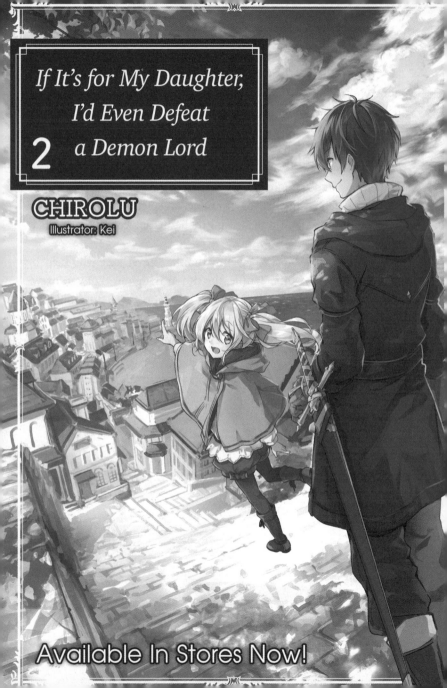

How NOT to Summon a Demon Lord

VOLUMES 1-3
ON SALE NOW!

In Another World With My Smartphone

©Patora Fuyuhara, Illustration: Eiji Usatsuka

novel club

HEY///////
▶ **HAVE YOU HEARD OF**
J-Novel Club?

It's the digital publishing company that brings you the latest novels from Japan!

Subscribe today at

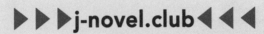

▶ ▶ ▶**j-novel.club**◀ ◀ ◀

and read the latest volumes as they're translated, or become a premium member to get a *FREE* ebook every month!

Check Out The Latest Volume Of
If It's For My Daughter, I'd Even Defeat a Demn Lord

Plus Our Other Hit Series Like:

- ▶ The Master of Ragnarok & Blesser of Eihenjar
- ▶ Invaders of the Rokujouma!?
- ▶ Grimgar of Fantasy and Ash
- ▶ Outbreak Company
- ▶ Amagi Brilliant Park
- ▶ Kokoro Connect
- ▶ Seirei Gensouki: Spirit Chronicles

...and many more!

- ▶ The Faraway Paladin
- ▶ Arifureta: From Commonplace to World's Strongest
- ▶ In Another World With My Smartphone
- ▶ How a Realist Hero Rebuilt the Kingdom
- ▶ Infinite Stratos
- ▶ Lazy Dungeon Master
- ▶ Sorcerous Stabber Orphen
- ▶ An Archdemon's Dilemma: How to Love Your Elf Bride

In Another World With My Smartphone, Illustration © Eiji Usatsuka   *Arifureta: From Commonplace to World's Strongest,* Illustration © Takayaki

J-Novel Club Lineup

Ebook Releases Series List

Amagi Brilliant Park
An Archdemon's Dilemma: How to Love Your Elf Bride
Ao Oni
Arifureta Zero
Arifureta: From Commonplace to World's Strongest
Bluesteel Blasphemer
Brave Chronicle: The Ruinmaker
Clockwork Planet
Demon King Daimaou
Der Werwolf: The Annals of Veight
ECHO
From Truant to Anime Screenwriter: My Path to "Anohana" and "The Anthem of the Heart"
Gear Drive
Grimgar of Fantasy and Ash
How a Realist Hero Rebuilt the Kingdom
How NOT to Summon a Demon Lord
I Saved Too Many Girls and Caused the Apocalypse
If It's for My Daughter, I'd Even Defeat a Demon Lord
In Another World With My Smartphone
Infinite Dendrogram
Infinite Stratos
Invaders of the Rokujouma!?
JK Haru is a Sex Worker in Another World
Kokoro Connect
Last and First Idol
Lazy Dungeon Master
Me, a Genius? I Was Reborn into Another World and I Think They've Got the Wrong Idea!
Mixed Bathing in Another Dimension
My Big Sister Lives in a Fantasy World
My Little Sister Can Read Kanji
My Next Life as a Villainess: All Routes Lead to Doom!
Occultic;Nine
Outbreak Company
Paying to Win in a VRMMO
Seirei Gensouki: Spirit Chronicles
Sorcerous Stabber Orphen: The Wayward Journey
The Faraway Paladin
The Magic in this Other World is Too Far Behind!
The Master of Ragnarok & Blesser of Einherjar
The Unwanted Undead Adventurer
Walking My Second Path in Life
Yume Nikki: I Am Not in Your Dream

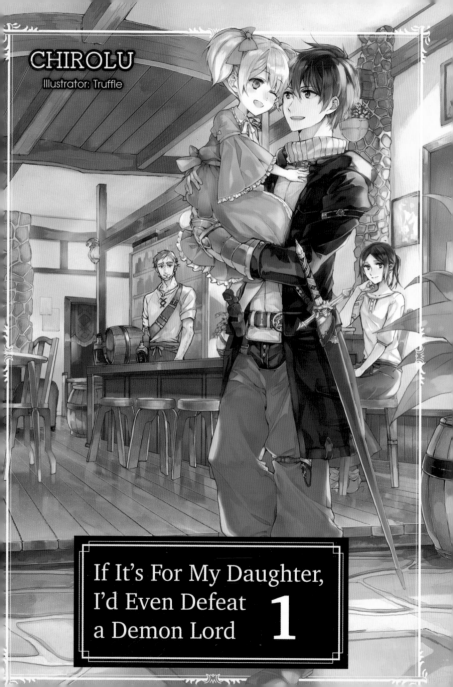

DALE REKI

A YOUNG MAN WHO HAS BECOME LATINA'S NEW GUARDIAN. WHEN IT COMES TO LATINA, THIS SKILLED ADVENTURER IS STUPIDLY IN LOVE WITH BEING A FATHER!

RITA KRUEGER

KENNETH'S WIFE, WHO HELPS RUN THE DANCING OCELOT. HER BEAUTY ATTRACTS CUSTOMERS TO THE BAR. SHE'S FOND OF CHILDREN, SO SHE CHERISHES LATINA'S PRESENCE.

KENNETH KRUEGER

THE OWNER OF THE DANCING OCELOT, THE BAR WHERE DALE ROOMS. ALONG WITH HIS WIFE, HE WATCHES OVER DALE'S AND LATINA'S DAY-TO-DAY LIVES.

"I LOVE YOU, LATINA."

"LATINA LOVES DALE BEST OF ALL..."

EVEN IF IT WAS JUST A BIT, SHE BROKE OUT IN A SMILE, MAKING HIM FEEL INCREDIBLY RELIEVED. FOR THAT SMILE, HE'D BE ABLE TO WORK HARDER THAN HE EVER HAD BEFORE. THAT'S WHAT HE THOUGHT FROM THE BOTTOM OF HIS HEART.